EX LIBRIS

VINTAGE CLASSICS

A French Christmas

Festive Tales for a Joyeux Noël

VINTAGE

1 3 5 7 9 10 8 6 4 2

Vintage Classics is part of the Penguin Random House group of companies
whose addresses can be found at global.penguinrandomhouse.com

Penguin
Random House
UK

First published in the United States of America as
A Very French Christmas by New Vessel Press in 2017
First published in Great Britain as *A French Christmas*
by Vintage Classics in 2024

penguin.co.uk/vintage-classics

Typeset in 12/15 pt Bembo Book MT Pro by Jouve (UK), Milton Keynes
Printed and bound in Great Britain by Clays Ltd, Elcograf S.p.A.

The authorised representative in the EEA is Penguin Random House Ireland,
Morrison Chambers, 32 Nassau Street, Dublin D02 YH68

A CIP catalogue record for this book is available from the British Library

ISBN 9781784879914

Penguin Random House is committed to a sustainable future
for our business, our readers and our planet. This book is made
from Forest Stewardship Council® certified paper.

Contents

CONTENTS

THE GIFT

Jean-Philippe Blondel

To be honest, I've always loathed Christmas.

Of course, it was a bit different when the children were little and ran around the house clapping their hands, but that didn't last too long. They quickly realised that Father Christmas didn't exist and that this was just an occasion to get or to try to get things they had been wanting for the past several months. The ideal moment for being angry or sullen because they didn't receive exactly what they had 'ordered'. There's nothing like the verb 'to order' to evoke the year-end holidays for me.

But I'm being unfair to them. It didn't start with their birth, but well before. With my own childhood. My father, who was promoted within his company soon after my arrival on earth, had to move for his new position. My parents didn't know anyone in the large provincial town where they were to establish themselves. My grandparents lived far away; they were old and in poor health. We didn't have guests over on the night before Christmas, or New Year's Eve. We'd hear the neighbours celebrating one floor below. And above us as well. And next door. We were surrounded by party hats and horns. We'd unwrap slices of cellophane-sealed salmon. We cut up the frozen lamb. We savored *bûche de Noël* bought at the supermarket. All in semi-religious silence, my brother, my mother, my father and me. One might have thought I'd find comfort in my older brother, but we were six years apart in age and he always wanted to escape from this hellish silence, which he finally managed to do very early, leaving me to endure as well I could the meals, the weekends, the holidays and the end of year celebrations.

Hélène, on the other hand, adored Christmas. She had the enthusiasm of a little girl, spending hours debating the decoration of the tree (should it be blue and silver or red and gold this year?), baking cookies, buying Advent calendars, chocolates and spices for mulled wine.

It's because of her that our children love Christmas — there's no doubt about that. After the divorce, of course, things got slightly complicated. The children, who were adults by then, bent themselves out of shape to not leave their father or mother alone for Christmas Eve or Day. Thibault, the eldest, usually arranged to be with my ex-wife the evening of the 24th and would come to spend the next day with me, while Isabelle and Pierre, the younger ones, did the opposite. Of course, when they each married and had their own children, that all became unmanageable and family gatherings got more haphazard – I certainly didn't complain about it. Thibault, who for years had been a financial advisor, began to hate his job and suddenly threw it aside to realise his dream of opening a restaurant. But not just any restaurant: typically French cuisine, with locally grown products, all organic. Thibault wanted us to inaugurate his establishment all together the following Christmas – father, mother, offspring, uncles, aunts, cousins – the clan in all its splendour. Hélène's heart attack on December 22nd changed all that. She was buried four days later. She was sixty-seven years old. By that time, we'd already been divorced for two decades. We hadn't seen each other for several months. Following these events, it was decided at a family meeting from which I was evidently excluded that on each and every December 25th, the entire family would now have lunch at Thibault's restaurant – *La Tambouille* – the name meant Chow – so that the living could celebrate, open their presents together and see joy spread over the faces of the youngest ones while also paying homage to the deceased mother.

It's now the twelfth Christmas since my ex-wife's death. I'm seventy-nine years old. I'm still in decent shape. Even if my hearing is showing signs of fatigue, my vision is still excellent and I still regularly do fifteen minutes of exercise daily as well as one or two walks a day. Nevertheless, we know – the children, grandchildren and I – that I'm not immortal and that soon, on the 25th, they'll also be honouring my memory.

Like every year for the past dozen, I'm waiting for them. They have to come pick up 'Grandpa'. Pierre and Isabelle will probably be in charge because Thibault is busy in the kitchen with his staff. He decided a few years ago that the restaurant should open for lunch on the twenty-fifth. To be sure, we won't be the only guests, thereby combining the beneficial (that's to say the profitable) with the pleasurable (his idea of a family gathering is one where he makes only periodic appearances since he's occupied in the kitchen). We thought the idea was doomed to fail (who after all was going to go out for lunch at a restaurant at noon on December 25th?) but it turned out to be extremely sound. The place is totally packed each year, with tables booked up sometimes six months in advance. Pierre and Isabelle, then, and without doubt one or two members of the third generation, those adorable kids who gradually transform themselves into brooding, unpleasant adolescents and then into impertinent and ironical adults. As always, 'Grandpa' gets put in the passenger seat, known as the 'death spot', perhaps betraying a secret desire on their part, even if they all find me endearing, to see me gone and buried so they can divvy up their inheritance; it seems I'm much richer than I appear and that, thanks to well advised investments, I've managed to amass a small fortune. They've casually tried to ask me about this. I've said nothing to confirm or deny the rumour. They tell 'Grandpa' how happy they are to see him in good form; they shower him with charming, bland smiles, telling him about the latest exploits of the youngest grandchildren and bringing him up to date on the brilliant careers of the eldest. They remind him of the names of the first great grandchildren. And then in the end, when there's not much of a response beyond a grunt or a gurgle, they lean back in their seats saying that 'Grandpa' isn't so easygoing, he always had a difficult character and that doesn't change with age, he could still be a bit more polite and show a little more gratitude towards this family that spends Christmas Day with him; he barely smiles, it's true, which seems to prove that he doesn't enjoy it and that we organise the whole hoopla for nothing, he'd rather stay at home near the radiator with a book; ah yes, books, for 'Grandpa', you'd think they were more important than human beings.

How can they possibly know such things? No member of this family reads novels, except for mass-market bestsellers, clichéd thrillers with contrived plots, idiotic romances or discounted pseudoeroticism. And so forth. They drag the books around with them during the summer, glancing at a few lines and then quickly going back to their preferred activities – catching up on the latest gossip and convincing themselves that the life they've chosen is better than it is. Voilà. The absence of literature, among my children, is the most crushing failure of my existence. It's not yours, Hélène, I know. You used to reproach my passion for reading. My dilettantism – you used to say there are so many other more interesting and certainly more useful things to do – fixing things around the house, rearranging the furniture, laundry, cooking. Don't misunderstand me. I did my share of household chores, you can't say otherwise, but it was never enough. And above all, you started to detest books. But that wasn't the case at the beginning. We'd finished our respective studies, you always had a novel in your purse, even if you didn't open it too often. I don't know what happened to us, Hélène. Or rather, I do. The kids soaked up our energy and our sense of self. We devoted all our time to them. We were happy to let them devour us. But you see, it's excruciating, isn't it, while I'm waiting for them here on the sofa twelve years after your death and probably for not too much longer, while I'm sighing at the idea of losing my first name and my personality to become 'Grandpa', because now even Pierre, Isabelle and Thibault call me 'Grandpa' and no longer 'Papa', just as I began to call you 'Maman' instead of using your first name; people ought to pay attention to those vocabulary shifts since they're indicative of the real turn of events – while I'm waiting for them and close my eyes as I listen out for the honking of the horn announcing their arrival, I wonder if we were right.

Absolutely.

Because the wild part of me, that part that frightened and delighted you at the start of our relationship, the part that you swore to tame and that you managed to subdue until, realising that a certain routine had become our existence, you began to be bored to death and to find our union so dull that you opted to file for divorce – that part of me that defined me as much as my other, more refined side, more consensual, the lover of books and fine liquors, the midlevel manager of a textile company, a pretty boy who was a bit too affable, that part, I believe I've lost. And when you lose part of your identity, you already have one foot in the grave. Don't worry, the other three will follow soon.

I still talk to you, you see, Hélène. Even though our divorce was finalised thirty-two years ago. Even though after you, there was Lydia, that shapely redhead who you became jealous of when we separated. And then Ludmilla. Olivia. Anne. Elisabeth. Five women in thirty-two years. Two women with whom, in contrast to you, I stayed on good terms. It has to be said that the stakes weren't the same. We were adults, immune, parents, we knew life wasn't a bed of roses. I meet them sometimes for lunch or dinner. We get along well. I don't have the slightest regret. In any case, in my emotional life, I have no regrets. And that includes you, for sure, Hélène. I'm happy to have shared all those years with you. Well, perhaps not those last five.

Sorry?

Who?

Ah, yes, okay.

One.

I have one regret.

Only one. In seventy-nine years of life. I can't complain. There. I hear the horn honking. It's time for me to turn into 'Grandpa', Hélène. Leave me.

One p.m. Still two hours to go and then I can pretend I'm exhausted and they'll take me home. I try to put on a good face. I smile when spoken to – it's one of the rare things that connect me to youth – smiling. I've always taken care of my teeth and they're still in astonishingly good condition for my age. Two implants, a bridge, the rest are original. Their colour hasn't been too spoiled by the cigarettes I smoked with punishing regularity for three decades until stopping abruptly at age fifty. That hasn't prevented me from dreaming of taking a puff once in a while – and even from imagining that I smell cigarette smoke in the midst of this group of non-smokers who make up my family and who speak about me in the third person. The stilted thanks, the fake cries of pleasure, the obligatory joy. I join in. I don't want them to reproach me for spoiling their day. But when I open the packages, I nearly faint. A pair of socks, a bathrobe, a comb; items fit for the hospital or retirement home. Jonas, one of my less irritating grandsons, gave me a watch, a rather ugly metal watch, true, but still it was a present you might receive at any age. Evidently, no one managed to buy me a novel because, as Chantal, Thibault's wife, declared, 'You're hard to buy for, Grandpa, you've read them all, and who knows what you'd like.' It wouldn't have occurred to anybody to ask me ahead of time for a list, for example. An old guy has no desires, that's well known. And plus to give me a novel, that would mean going into the centre of town, walking into a bookshop – it doesn't take much more than that. You could buy one at a superstore, but Grandpa doesn't like novels from superstores, it seems. He's difficult, Grandpa.

The restaurant is full. It's been transformed for the occasion. Instead of twenty tables of four or six, there are five large tables – five families gathered to share a convivial moment. Three of them are regulars. They make an appearance here every December 25. The fourth, no. New people.

9

They're a bit less numerous than we are, but they're still a good dozen. Two daughters, their husbands, the grandchildren, two or three in-laws, and then, presiding over the assembly, a woman with white hair. The grandfather must have given up the ghost. Men generally resist less well than their spouses. I'm observing her. Her slightly absent look. The smile floating on her lips. She's bored as well. She feels a bit guilty since she should feel great, there with all her family – but she suppresses a yawn. She'd rather be elsewhere. She's no longer used to long meals. She never liked them, by the way. I realise that I'm trying to invent a life for her. That's the problem with literature. One narrates. One embroiders. One adds material.

It's at this moment she turns her head slightly towards me and our eyes meet.

I hear a faint explosion far away. It's like a summer storm in the middle of winter, or the start of fireworks whose noise is muffled by the distance. I can't take myself away from her gaze. My memory has turned into a crazy machine, searching all my internal libraries for the relevant novel, and in this heap of cards and photographs that we store inside ourselves, the information that I need is right there. Because I know her.

I'm sure I know her.

But I don't recognise her.

I realise that my breath is short and my heart is beating fast – I blush a bit and chuckle. I totally chuckle. At the other end of the room, she narrows her eyes and silently pronounces my name, Thomas; I nod, she too, more slowly. My body panics. I wonder if I'm not going to die there in the middle of a Christmas celebration, from a heart attack whose cause will remain unknown to them, just as they are unaware of my inner compartments, my trajectory, my youth, my life before their mother and with their mother prior to their births, those days of snow or heat waves when our bodies remained entwined and we couldn't suppress our desire.

My hand on her shoulder.

My young hand on her naked shoulder.

My young hand that slowly unfastens the white bra to unveil this naked shoulder with three moles at the base of the shoulder blade.

Three moles. Hélène didn't have any in that place. I close my eyes. I see a purple neon sign in the street, a bit farther away, with a cocktail glass and a straw in the shape of a parasol, the Relax Cocktail Lounge, the name comes back to me now. There was an evening get-together, organised by the company executives, 'Come on, Thomas,' they said. 'You'll see. It's really nice, the atmosphere is subdued and the hostesses are obliging.' Hearty laughter. I was embarrassed for her.

Alice.

There, that's her name. Alice. Alice Leprince.

She was the only woman in management at Fabre & Sons, and evidently they didn't think for an instant that their smutty undertone could offend her. I think that actually she didn't exist for them, she served solely as an example and a counterexample when one reproached them for their retrograde attitude towards women. 'But that's absurd!' thundered the director. 'Look at Alice! She's in charge of exports, isn't that right, Alice?' Tight smiles. She didn't stay long. She resigned. She left for the competitor. I never got any news. For a while, yes, I regretted it.

Because there was that moment, suspended. A parenthesis. I had of course promised my colleagues and my superiors that I'd join them at the Relax, but first I had to stretch a little bit, I had a bad back. I'd thought of using headaches as an excuse, but they would have laughed – migraines, that's feminine, that's what a woman resorts to when she doesn't want to make love; migraines are degrading and ridiculous. The back, that's good. It's a perfect manly excuse. Lots of weight to carry around, lots of responsibilities and then typically male activity; cutting wood, assembling furniture, spending hours under the hood of a car, and suddenly you find yourself folded in half from lumbago. Yes, definitely, back pain, that's just what was needed, especially since everyone knew I had a double herniated disc, I broadcast it everywhere when I came back from being seen at the doctor's. Everybody sympathised. No one checked. I knew that a double herniated disc would be useful to me later. They left in a hubbub of insolence and dirty jokes. Alice Leprince came down a few minutes later. She recoiled slightly upon seeing me and then she put her hand over her mouth, to apologise for this fright that she shouldn't have had.

'You didn't go with them?'

'No, I . . . I told them a white lie: back pain.'

She raised an eyebrow. I didn't understand what made me, all of a sudden, confess to her the truth that I hid from the others.

'White lie?'

'Yes, it's made up. But I didn't feel like . . . In the end, you know . . . hostesses, alcohol, raunchy stories . . . sorry . . . I don't want you to think I'm better than them, I . . .'

'But you are.'

'Sorry?'

'Better than them. You are. Undeniably.'

'That's not what they think.'

'They don't think anything, Thomas. The only thing that interests them is their own careers. And money. Take me, for instance: they think I'm a dummy who needs to be ravished in order to let loose.'

I recall the heat on my face. I wasn't as free as her. I wasn't used to a woman talking like that. Hélène wasn't so crude. Hélène adhered to the norm.

'I think I'm going to take a walk in town. Along the river, apparently it's beautiful.'

'It's going to be dark soon.'

'Exactly. Do you want to join me?'

Such boldness was new for me, an audacity that pushed me to invite a woman I barely knew to join me for an evening walk. I wasn't the type of man capable of such things. I had a good life; I was a father and a loving husband absorbed in work, a creature of habit whose children made fun of him at times because his rituals were immutable, a prisoner for whom books were the sole diversion – a passion shared by no one around me. And suddenly, with Alice Leprince, I entered into one of those secret novels that frightened and attracted me at the same time. I rediscovered a part of adolescence as well, before my path had already been decided, before bumpy roads became smooth highways.

That's how we ended up alongside the river, Alice Leprince and me. She very quickly confided her thoughts to me, by the way. Not just about other companies, but other cities, countries, horizons. She felt she couldn't remain here for too long. She'd leave Fabre & Sons fairly soon. We talked for hours; there were times we said nothing. I hadn't done that in years. It was as if all barriers had fallen away. In the middle of the night we returned separately to the hotel. She went first. I came back ten minutes later. We were afraid we'd run into our colleagues. We were wrong. They'd already come back. The evening at the Relax had turned out to be disappointing.

My hand on her shoulder.

My hand that slowly unfastens the white bra to unveil this naked shoulder with three moles at the base of the shoulder blade.

I was thirty-nine. She was thirty-three.

I remember all the details. They come to me sometimes at night. I drift from one dream to another and suddenly, she's a fleeting apparition in a crowd, I run to find her, I cry out that I'm free now, have been free for a while, but she's caught up in movement and disappears. I sigh. I'm used to it. I think I'll chase after this chimera until I die.

After my divorce, I tried to find Alice Leprince, even if I imagined her throwing open shutters overlooking the Grand Canal or the temples of Kyoto, an indefatigable adventurer, a freelance journalist, a talent scout. In fact, around the year 2000, I even learned how to use a computer and the Internet for the sole purpose of locating her. But women, by marrying and taking their husband's last name, can easily erase their earthly traces. I quickly understood that it was wasted effort. Then, there were other interests, other novels, other goals, some travelling, health concerns, family worries, five successive women with whom I shared daily life and age that advances and gnaws. I forgot Alice Leprince.

And then suddenly, she's there – so different and yet unmistakable. Four decades later. One often believes that when you get older you won't recognise those you knew when you were young, but that's not true. It's totally not true. Sure, the skin has withered, the smile is parched, there are wrinkles, but the face stays the same and the general allure doesn't change that much in the end. Nor does desire. When she silently mouthed my first name, this name that no one had spoken at this table since I became Grandpa, a Grandpa like all the other Grandpas, a Grandpa without an identity, and when her lips formed 'Thomas', my throat became dry and my hands tingled. She froze for a few seconds, knitted her eyebrows, then furtively nodded her head towards the restaurant entrance. My heart didn't stop pounding. I complied. The members of her family didn't see anything. Mine either. A few seconds later, I saw her speak to the person sitting next to her – her daughter? – and move towards the restroom, shooting me a discrete, meaningful look. I coughed. I confided to Pierre, who was to my right, that I had a pressing need and I'd be back in a minute. He wanted to accompany me but I satisfied him with a 'and what for?' that kept him from getting up. I sensed a twitching in my muscles and under my skin, as if suddenly I'd returned to life. No one paid attention to us. Grandma. Grandpa. We're so insignificant in this world oriented towards youth. We found ourselves face-to-face in front of the restrooms. She smiled. I asked her at this point if I was ugly. She shook her head. She apologised. She explained that that's the way it is, it's so . . .

'Unexpected?'

'Unexpected, no. More like not something I thought would actually happen. I knew that your son had taken over the restaurant. I dragged my family here several times in the hope of finding you. I knew you were still alive.'

'You could have just come to my house.'

She shrugged her shoulders, told me that she'd done that a few times over the past few months, but had never dared to ring the bell, or call. She was afraid. Of everything. That I wouldn't recognise her. That I would be blind, deaf, on a respirator. Or worse, a victim of Alzheimer's.

'I remember you so well, Alice. You're my only regret.'

Her hand stroked mine. The effect was immediate. I felt myself blush to the roots of my hair. She passed a hand through my hair. She suggested that we take a walk by the river.

'What river?'

'There's one nearby, no? If not, we'll go a little farther.'

'It's winter, Alice.'

'Do you lack imagination at this stage?'

'I've always been that way.'

'I'm not sure of that. Will you join me?'

'On foot?'

'Let's not overdo it. In a few minutes, we'll be frozen. How about you take your car?'

I sigh. I reply that I haven't driven in ages. She smiles again – lighting up this sordid setting, the entryway to the restrooms in a restaurant called La Tambouille, deep in the French provinces, a day of mandatory libations. She transforms it into a rugged landscape overlooking the Mediterranean, a steep road in the Alps.

'Very well, we'll take mine. I've always liked driving. Wait ten minutes, I'll go get the keys.'

I cast a nervous glance at the family table. I'm not afraid that they'll be upset their Christmas has been ruined. No. I fear that they'll interfere. That they'll deprive us of this last bit of freedom. I needn't be so worried. They're involved in heated conversations mixing politics, TV, social media and celebrities. They're not paying attention to me.

I see Alice say a few words to her daughter, smile, touch her arm, and surreptitiously grab her purse. And as she walks along the wall of the restaurant to rejoin me, I hear your voice, Hélène, and it overwhelms me.

THE GIFT

I guessed it, you see.
I suspected you were behind all this.
It's your gift, isn't it? For my last Christmas?
Thank you, Hélène.
A thousand times, thank you.

2017

ST ANTHONY AND HIS PIG

Paul Arène

St Anthony pushed open the door and saw in his cabin half a dozen little children who had come up from the village, in spite of the storm, to bring him some honey and nuts, dainties which the good hermit allowed himself to enjoy once a year, on Christmas Day, on account of his great age.

'Sit around the fire, friends, and throw on two or three pine knots to make a blaze. That's right. Now make room for Barrabas; poor, faithful Barrabas, who is so cold that his tail is all out of curl.'

The children coughed and wiped their noses, and Barrabas – for that is the real name of St Anthony's pig – Barrabas grunted, with his feet comfortably buried in the warm ashes.

The saint threw back his hood, shook the snow from his shoulders, passed his hand over his long grey beard, all hung with little icicles, and having seated himself, began:

'So you want me to tell you about my temptation?'

'Yes, good St Anthony; yes, kind St Anthony.'

'My temptation? But you know as much as I do about my temptation. It has been drawn and painted a thousand times, and you can see on my wall – God forgive me this piece of vanity – all the *prints*, old and new, dedicated to my glory and that of Barrabas; from Épinal's sketch which costs a sou including the song, to the admirable masterpieces of Teniers, Breughel, and Callot.

'I am sure your mothers must have taken you to the marionnette theatre at Luxembourg, to see my poor hermitage, just as it is here, with the chapel, the cabin, the bell hanging in the crotch of a tree, and myself at prayer, while Proserpine offers me a cup, and a host of little devils dancing at the end of a string are tormenting and terrifying poor Barrabas.

'After a while, when you have learned to read, you will see behind the glass doors of your father's bookcase these words:

'*The Temptation of St Anthony*, by Gustave Flaubert, in letters of gold on the back of a handsome book.

'This M. Flaubert is a clever fellow, though he does not write for little children like you, and what he says about me is all very true. The artists, of whom I spoke to you just now, have not omitted any of the devils which have tormented me at different times; in fact, they have added a few.

'That is the reason, my children, that I am afraid I should weary you if I should tell you again things that you already know so well.'

'Oh, St Anthony! Oh, good St Anthony!'

'Let me tell you something else –'

'No, no; the temptation, the temptation!'

'Well, well,' said St Anthony, 'I see that I shall not escape the temptation this year; but as you have been unusually good, I will tell you about one which no artist has ever painted, and which M. Flaubert knows nothing about. Nevertheless it was a terrible temptation – was it not, Barrabas? – and kept me a long time on the slope at whose foot the fires of hell are glowing.

'It was at midnight, just such a night as this, that the thing occurred.'

At this beginning, Barrabas, evidently interested, raised himself on his two front feet to listen, the children shivered and drew closer together, and here is the Christmas story which the good saint told them:

'Well, my friends, I must tell you that after a thousand successive temptations, the devils, all at once, stopped tormenting me. My nights were once more peaceful. No more monsters with horns and tails, carrying me through the air on their bat's wings; no more devil's imps with he-goat's beards and monkey faces; no more infernal musicians trying to frighten Barrabas, with their stomachs made of a double bass, and great noses which sounded like an unearthly clarion; no more Queen Proserpines in robes of gold and precious stones, graceful and majestic.

'And I said to myself, "All's well, Anthony; the devils are discouraged." Barrabas and I were as happy as we could be, on our rock.

'Barrabas followed me about everywhere, delighting me with his childish gaiety. As for me, I did what all good hermits do. I prayed, I rang my bell at the proper times, and between my prayers and offices, I drew water from the spring for the vegetables in my garden.

'This lasted six months or more; six delightful months of solitude.

'I slept in perfect security, but unhappily the Evil One was still awake.

'One day, near Christmastime, I was about to sun myself in my doorway, when a man presented himself. He wore hobnailed shoes and a square-cut velvet coat, and carried on his back a pedlar's pack.

'He called out:

'"Spits, spits, spits! Buy some spits!" with a slight Auvergnese accent.

'"Do you want a spit, good hermit?"

'"Go your way, my good man. I live on cold water and roots and have no use for your spits."

'"All right, all right. I am only trying to sell my wares."

'"However," added he, with a fiendish glance at Barrabas, who, more sagacious than I, was grunting furiously in a corner, "however, that fellow there looks so fat and sleek, that I thought – God forgive me! that you might be keeping him for your Christmas Eve supper."

'The fact was that Barrabas, the rascal, had grown very fat, now that the devils no longer troubled his digestion.

'I suddenly became aware of this fact, but was far enough from any thought of feasting upon my only friend, so when I saw the pedlar go down the path, spit in hand, I could not help laughing at the idea. Little by little, however, like the growth of a noxious weed, the infernal idea – for it was evidently a devil from hell disguised as a pedlar, who had tried to sell me the spit – this infernal idea of eating Barrabas took root in my mind. I saw spits; I dreamed of spits. In vain I increased my mortifications and penances. Penances and mortifications availed nothing, and fasting – fasting only seemed to sharpen my appetite.

'I avoided looking at Barrabas. I no longer dared take him with me on my expeditions, and when, at my return, he ran to rub the rough bristles on his back against my bare feet, I turned away my eyes right quickly and had not the heart to caress him.

'But I am afraid, children, that this does not interest you much and perhaps you would prefer –'

'No, good St Anthony!'

'Go on, kind St Anthony!'

'Well, then I will go on, however painful it may be to me to recall those terrible memories. What temptations! What trials! The devil often makes use of the most innocent things to lead a man astray.

'Near my hermitage there was a little wood (I think there are still a few trees there) where some good people had given me permission to take Barrabas to eat acorns.

'It was our favourite walk at sunset, when the oak leaves smell so good.

'I read, while Barrabas gorged himself with acorns, and often while he rooted about in the damp leaves, he turned up rough-looking black balls, which smelled very nice indeed, and these he ate greedily.'

'Perhaps they were truffles, good St Anthony.'

'Yes, my little friend, truffles; a cryptogamous plant which I had scorned till that time, but whose odour struck me all at once as very delicious and appetising.

'So that from that moment every time that Barrabas dug up a truffle, I made him drop it by hitting him a sharp blow on the snout with a stick, and then – wretched hypocrite that I was – threw him a chestnut or two so that he might not become discouraged.'

'Oh, St Anthony!'

'In that way I collected several pounds.'

'And you were going to cook Barrabas's feet with truffles?'

'Well, I had not altogether decided to do so, but I acknowledge I was thinking about it.

'Beside my door,' continued the hermit, 'a seed brought by the wind had sprouted and grown up between the rock and the wall. Its long leaves of a greyish green smelled very nice, and in the spring the bees came to steal honey from its little purple flowers. I loved this modest plant, which seemed to grow for me alone. I watered it. I cared for it. I put a little earth about its roots.

'But, alas, one morning as I broke off a little sprig and smelled it, I had a sudden and tempting vision of quarters of pork roasting on a spit, deluging with their golden gravy, bits of an herb thrust into the meat and shrivelling and curling in the heat of the fire. My plant, my modest little plant, was the sage so dear to cooks, and its savoury odour thenceforth called to mind only images of spareribs and roast pig. Ashamed of myself, I pulled up my sage, and gave all the truffles at once to Barrabas, who had a grand feast on them.

'But I was not to get off so cheaply. The sage pulled up, the truffles thrown away, my temptation still continued.

'They became more frequent, more irresistible as Christmastime approached.

'Put yourselves in my place: with a robust stomach, for years poorly nourished with roots and cold water, what I saw pass at the foot of my rock, on the high road which leads to the city, was well fitted to ruin a holier man than I. What a procession, my friends! The country people – good Christians as they were – were preparing for the Christmas Eve feast a week beforehand, and from morn till night nothing went by but eatables. Carts full of deer and wild boars, nets full of lobsters, hampers full of fish and oysters; cocks and hens hanging by their feet under the wagons; fat sheep going to the slaughterhouse; ducks and pheasants; a flock of squawking geese; turkeys shaking their crimson wattles; not to mention the good country women carrying baskets full of fruit ripened on straw, bunches of grapes, and white winter melons; eggs and milk for custards and creams; honey in the comb and in jars; cheeses and dried figs.

'And, greatest temptation of all, the despairing cries of some poor pig, tied by the leg and dragged squealing along.

'At last Christmas came. The Midnight Mass over at the hermitage, and everybody gone, I locked the chapel and shut myself up quickly in my hut. It was cold: as cold as it is today.

The north wind blew and the fields and roads were covered with snow. I heard laughing and singing outside. It was some of my parishioners who were going to eat their Christmas Eve feast in the neighbourhood. I looked through the hole in my shutter. Here and there over the white plain the bright fires shone out from the farmhouse windows, and down below the illuminated city sent up a glow to heaven, like the reflection from a great furnace. Then I called to mind the Christmas Eve feasts of my gormandising youth. My grandfather presiding at the table, and christening with new wine the great backlog. I saw the smoking dishes, the white tablecloth, the firelight dancing on the pewter pots and platters on the dresser; and at the thought of myself alone with Barrabas, when all the world was feasting, sitting before a miserable fire, with a jug of water and a wretched root, a sudden sadness seized me. I cried, "What a Christmas feast," and burst into tears.

'The tempter was only waiting for this moment.

'For the last few minutes the silence of the night had been broken by the sound of invisible wings. Then came a shout of laughter, and a series of discreet little knocks on door and shutter.

'"The devils! Hide, hide, Barrabas!" cried I, and Barrabas, who had good reason to hate all sorts of devilish tricks, took refuge behind the kneading trough.

'The slates on my roof rattled as if it were hailing. The infernal gang was once more let loose about my head.

'But now we come to the strangest thing. Instead of the terrific noises and discords by which my enemies generally announced their coming – cries of foul night-birds, bleating of he-goats, rattling of bones, and clanking of iron chains – this time they were low sounds; at first quite vague, like those which the chilly traveller hears from out an inn whose doors are closed, and which, growing more and more distant, resolve themselves into a marvellous music of turning of spits, stirring of saucepans, clinking of glasses, emptying of bottles, rattling of forks and plates, and sizzling of frying pans.

'All at once the music ceased. The walls of my cabin trembled, the shutter blew open, the door slammed back, and the wind, rushing in, put out my lamp.

'I expected to smell brimstone and sulphur. But, no! Not at all! This time the infernal wind was laden with pleasant odours of burned sugar and cinnamon. My cabin smelled very sweet.

'Just then I heard a squeal from Barrabas. They had found out his hiding place.

'"Come, come," said I, "the old jokes are beginning again. They are going to tie fireworks on his tail once more." These devils have not much invention. And forgetting myself, I prayed Heaven to grant my companion strength to bear the trial. But as he cried louder and louder, I ventured to open my eyes, and my lamp being suddenly relighted, I saw the unfortunate martyr held fast by his tail and his ears, and struggling for dear life, surrounded by white devils.'

'White devils! Good St Anthony!'

'Yes, my friends, white devils. The very whitest of the white, I assure you, disguised as they were as scullions and potboys, in short jackets and caps. They brandished larding needles and pranced about with dripping-pans.

'However, in the middle of the room they had placed a long board on two trestles, and on this they stretched Barrabas. Near the board was a big knife, a pail, a little broom, and a sponge. Barrabas squealed, and I knew that they were about to cut his throat.

'What a soul-destroying thing is gluttony! While the blood was running and Barrabas was still squealing, my soul was greatly disquieted. But Barrabas once silent – "Bah," said I to myself, "since he is dead" – and with guilty coolness and even with a certain interest, I looked at Barrabas in the hands of the assassins. The innocent Barrabas, the dear companion of my solitude, cruelly torn to pieces and marvellously transformed into a multitude of savoury things.

'I saw him cut open, cleaned and scraped, hung by the feet along a ladder, washed as white as a lily, and smelling very good already in the steam of the boiling water; then cut, chopped, salted, made into sausages, pâté meat, all with diabolical rapidity; so that in a twinkling my hearthstone was covered with a bed of live coals (the devils are never at a loss for anything). I was surrounded by steaming kettles, gridirons, and spits, where, amid perfumes as fragrant as ambergris, in gravies and sauces ruddy as gold, bubbled, sizzled, fried, boiled – and that, I confess, to my great joy and satisfaction – the remains of him who was my friend, now transformed into pork.

'All of a sudden everything changes. What a spectacle! A palace instead of a cabin; no more cooking and no more live coals. The broken walls were hung with tapestry; the floor of beaten earth was covered with a carpet.

'Only the slates of the roof kept their places, but these were transformed into a wonderful vine trellis, and through their openings were seen the blue sky and the stars. I had already admired one like it at the house of a rich man in the city, where I had preached repentance for sin. And through these openings ascended and descended a host of little scullions carrying dishes, catching on by the brittle vine twigs, sliding down the branches and covering a table beside me with meats done to a turn.

'There was everything on that table. Ah! My friends, my mouth waters at the thought – Stop, what was I going to say?

No; at the very thought of it, my heart is full of remorse. Four hams, two big and two little; four truffled feet; only one head, but stuffed so full of pistachio nuts; steaks; galantines blushing through their mantle of quivering amber jelly; dainty forcemeat balls; twisted sausages; puddings black as hell.

'Then the roasts; the hashes; the sauces; and I, with staring eyes and dilated nostrils, wondered that so many savoury things could be contained under the bristles of a humble animal, and my heart ached at the thought of poor Barrabas.'

'But did you eat any of him?'

'Almost. I almost ate some, my friends. I had already stuck my fork into the crackling skin of a black blood-pudding, offered me by a very polite little devil. The fork was in; the devil smiled.

'"Get thee behind me, get thee behind me!" cried I. I had just recognised the smile of the diabolical little pedlar, the cause of all my temptations, who two months before had tried to sell me a spit. "Get thee behind me, Satan!"

'The vision fled: it was daybreak and my fire had just gone out. Barrabas, well and happy, shook himself and rang the little bell about his neck, and instead of a host of white devils, snowflakes as big as your fist whirled in the door and window, which the storm had burst open.'

'And what next?' said the children, eager for more of the beautiful story.

'Next, my dear friends, with a heart full of penitence, I shared my meal of roots with Barrabas, and since then no more devils have ever come to disturb our Christmas Eve feast.'

1880

THE LOUIS D'OR

François Coppée

When Lucien de Hem saw his last bill for a hundred francs clawed by the banker's rake, when he rose from the roulette table where he had just lost the debris of his little fortune scraped together for this supreme battle, he experienced something like vertigo, and thought that he should fall. His brain was muddled; his legs were limp and trembling. He threw himself upon the leather lounge that circumscribed the gambling table. For a few moments he mechanically followed the clandestine proceedings of that hell in which he had sullied the best years of his youth, recognised the worn profiles of the gamblers under the merciless glare of the three great shadeless lamps, listened to the clicking and the sliding of the gold over the felt, realised that he was bankrupt, lost, remembered that in the top drawer of his dressing table lay a pair of pistols – the very pistols of which

General de Hem, his father, had made noble use at the attack of Zaatcha; then, overcome by exhaustion, he sank into a heavy sleep.

When he awoke his mouth was clammy, and his tongue stuck to his palate. He realised by a hasty glance at the clock that he had scarcely slept a half hour, and he felt the imperious necessity of going out to get a breath of the fresh night air. The hands on the dial pointed exactly to a quarter of twelve. As he rose and stretched his arms it occurred to him that it was Christmas Eve, and by one of those ironical freaks of the memory, he felt as though he were once more a child, ready to stand his little boot on the hearth before going to bed. Just then old Dronski, one of the pillars of the trade, the traditional Pole, wrapped in the greasy worn cloak adorned with frogs and passementerie, came up to Lucien muttering something behind his dirty grayish beard.

'Lend me five francs, will you, Monsieur? I haven't stirred from this place for two days, and for two whole days seventeen hasn't come out once. You may laugh at me all you like, but I bet you my fist that when the clock strikes twelve, seventeen will be the winning number.'

Lucien de Hem shrugged his shoulders; and fumbling through his pockets, he found that he had not even money enough to comply with that feature of gambling etiquette known among the frequenters of the establishment as 'the

Pole's hundred cents'. He passed into the antechamber, put on his hat and cloak, and disappeared down the narrow stairway with the agility of people who have a fever. During the four hours which Lucien had spent in the den it had snowed heavily, and the street, one of those narrow wedges between two rows of high buildings in the very heart of Paris, was intensely white. Above, in the calm blue black of the sky, cold stars glittered. The exhausted gambler shivered under his furs, and hurried along with a blank despair in his heart, thinking of the pistols that awaited him in the top drawer of his dressing table. He had not gone a hundred feet when he stopped suddenly before a heart-rending spectacle.

On a stone bench, near the monumental doorway of a wealthy residence, sat a little girl six or seven years old, barely covered by a ragged black gown. She had fallen asleep there in spite of the bitter cold, her body bent forward in a pitiful posture of resigned exhaustion. Her poor little head and her dainty shoulder had moulded themselves into the angle of the freezing wall. One of her worn slippers had fallen from her dangling foot and lay in the snow before her. Lucien de Hem mechanically thrust his hand into his vest pocket, but he remembered that he had not even been able to fee the club waiter. He went up to the child, however, impelled by an instinct of pity. He meant, no doubt, to pick her up and take her home with him, to give her shelter for the night, when suddenly he saw something glitter in the little slipper at his feet. He stooped. It was a louis d'or.

Some charitable soul – a woman, no doubt – had passed there, and at the pathetic sight of that little shoe in the snow had remembered the poetic Christmas legend, and with discreet fingers had dropped a splendid gift, so that the forsaken little one might still believe in the presents of the Child Christ, and might awaken with renewed faith in the midst of her misery. A gold louis! That meant many days of rest and comfort for the little beggar. Lucien was just about to awaken her and surprise her with her good fortune when, in a strange hallucination, he heard a voice in his ear, which whispered with the drawling inflection of the old Pole: 'I haven't stirred from this place for two days, and for two whole days seventeen hasn't come out once. I'll bet you my fist that when the clock strikes twelve, seventeen will be the winning number.'

Then this youth, who was twenty-three years of age, the descendant of a race of honest men – this youth who bore a great military name, and had never been guilty of an unmanly act – conceived a monstrous thought; an insane desire took possession of him. He looked anxiously up and down the street, and having assured himself that he had no witness, he knelt, and reaching out cautiously with trembling fingers, stole the treasure from the little shoe, then rose with a spring and ran breathlessly down the street. He rushed like a madman up the stairs of the gambling house, flung open the door with his fist, and burst into the room at the first stroke of midnight. He threw the gold piece on the table and cried:

'Seventeen!'

Seventeen won. He then pushed the whole pile on the red. The red won. He left the seventy-two louis on the same colour. The red came out again. He doubled the stakes, twice, three times, and always with the same success. Before him was a huge pile of gold and banknotes. He tried the twelve, the column, he worked every combination. His luck was something unheard of, something almost supernatural. One might have believed that the little ivory ball, in its frenzied dance around the table, had been bewitched, magnetised by this feverish gambler, and obeyed his will. With a few bold strokes he had won back the bundle of banknotes which he had lost in the early part of the evening. Then he staked two and three hundred louis at a time, and as his fantastic luck never failed him, he soon won back the whole capital that had constituted his inherited fortune.

In his haste to begin the game he had not even thought of taking off his fur-lined coat, the great pockets of which were now swollen with the rolls of banknotes, and heavy with the weight of the gold. Not knowing where to put the money that was steadily accumulating before him, he stuffed it away in the inside and outside pockets of his coat, his vest, his trousers, in his cigar case, his handkerchief. Everything became a recipient. And still he played and still he won, his brain whirling the while like that of a drunkard or a madman. It was amazing to see him stand there throwing gold on the table by the handful, with that haughty gesture of absolute certainty and disdain. But withal there was a gnawing at his heart, something that felt like a red-hot iron there, and he could not rid himself of the vision of the child asleep in the snow, the child whom he had robbed.

'In just a few minutes,' said he, 'I will go back to her. She must be there in the same place. Of course she must be there. It is no crime, after all. I will make it right to her – it will be no crime. Quite the contrary. I will leave here in a few moments, when the clock strikes again, I swear it. Just as soon as the clock strikes again I will stop, I will go straight to where she is, I will take her up in my arms and will carry her home with me asleep. I have done her no harm; I have made a fortune for her. I will keep her with me and educate her; I will love her as I would a child of my own, and I will take care of her, always, as long as she lives!'

But the clock struck one, a quarter past, half past, and Lucien was still there. Finally, a few minutes before two the man opposite him rose brusquely and said in a loud voice, 'The bank is broken, gentlemen; this will do for tonight.'

Lucien started, and wedging his way brutally through the

group of gamblers, who pressed around him in envious admiration, hurried out into the street and ran as fast as he could towards the stone bench. In a moment he saw by the light of the gas that the child was still there.

'God be praised!' said he, and his heart gave a great throb of joy. Yes, here she was! He took her little hand in his. Poor little hand, how cold it was! He caught her under the arms and lifted her. Her head fell back, but she did not awake. 'The happy sleep of childhood!' thought he. He pressed her close to his breast to warm her, and with a vague presentiment he tried to rouse her from this heavy sleep by kissing her eyelids. But he realised then with horror that through the child's half-open lids her eyes were dull, glassy, fixed. A distracting suspicion flashed through his mind. He put his lips to the child's mouth; he felt no breath.

While Lucien had been building a fortune with the louis stolen from this little one, she, homeless and forsaken, had perished with cold.

Lucien felt a suffocating knot at his throat. In his anguish he tried to cry out, and in the effort which he made he awoke from his nightmare, and found himself on the leather lounge in the gambling room, where he had fallen asleep a little before midnight. The *garçon* of the den had gone home at about five o'clock, and out of pity had not wakened him.

A misty December dawn made the windowpanes pale.

Lucien went out, pawned his watch, took a bath, then went over to the Bureau of Recruits, and enlisted as a volunteer in the First Regiment of the *Chasseurs d'Afrique*.

Lucien de Hem is now a lieutenant. He has not a cent in the world but his pay. He manages to make that do, however, for he is a steady officer, and never touches a card. He even contrives to economise, it would seem; for a few days ago a comrade, who was following him up one of the steep streets of the Casbah, saw him stop to lay a piece of money in the lap of a little Spanish girl who had fallen asleep in a doorway. His comrade was startled at the poor lieutenant's generosity, for this piece of money was a gold louis.

1893

CHRISTMAS IN ALGIERS

Anatole Le Braz

I

The yule log sputtered softly, as if it had little old confidences to impart. And his feet to the flame, the soldier told stories in his slow tones, his hairy hands thrust in his blue belt – the kind the men of Leon wear.

He had, with all the regiment, served the campaign of Tunis at the double-quick. Of those others – a dozen of them Bretons like himself – more than one had stayed there, stretched out on his back in the great naked mountains, with a hole in his belly made by Khroumire bullets. And he added, in a tone of funereal humour, with the grave laugh that they have in the country of Saint-Thégonnek:

'It's a great while their bones have whitened surely, for the vultures that way make quick work of cleaning up a carcass.'

A voice spoke up: 'God rest their souls!'

He, at least, had returned – his skin blackened like an old harness, but without a cut. All the same, before seeing once more the chimney of his tiled cottage in the garden of Leon, he had had to serve his time below at the other side of the world, in 'Algiers of Africa'.

'You'd never believe,' he went on, wetting his lips in the bowl of warm cider, 'you would never believe with what a feeling of content I used to climb the twisty alleys of Casbah, where we had our barracks. It was exactly at Christmastime . . .'

'Ah, yes!' exclaimed the elder brother who had just taken holy orders and was to celebrate his first mass next day. 'You've told me of that Christmas!

'You know, between ourselves, you ought perhaps to make confession of it. It wasn't strictly orthodox.'

'Oh, my confession's easy enough,' he responded. 'Since you urge me on, I'll make it publicly.'

The Yuletide watchers cried out with one voice:

'That's it, Yvik! We'll absolve you. We all!'

The girls of the household poured into the bowls of painted clay a new round of the smoking cider. The soldier told his tale.

II

Well, on the twenty-fourth of December that you know about, he mounted guard in the Upper Town, happy to find himself there again, living and intact, whereas so many of his comrades . . . Enough!

Algiers is Africa, to be sure – but you can still smell the good odour of France. And he came and went, his gun at his shoulder.

At his feet, the white town melted into nothingness, like a great cascade of foam whipped by the wind as far as the dark blue of the sea. For a high wind was blowing. Down there, that is how the winter comes on. At every shifting of the squall, billows of water fell, and clouds raced madly across the troubled sky. And he took to placing them elsewhere, those clouds; and, in imagination, sketched out the ideal contour of another country, where their shadows moved over the ground as in procession . . .

Of what subtle substance is the Fatherland then made, that it too can travel, emigrating with us in agreement with our vagrant fantasies or our forced exiles? However far our destiny may take us, it seems as if always a little of it kept company with us, exhaling its fragrance wherever we pitch our tent. Something familiar in the face of a stranger passing, a scrap of song caught in a gust of wind, the shadow of a tree, the fugitive emanation of a perfume – less yet, a detail, a meaningless trifle, a nothing – and something within us sounds a mysterious call; a sudden combination works upon our most intimate essence – eliminates all that is contrasting, groups all that frames into the loved picture of the distant Fatherland. The Breton soul lends itself more readily than any other to this mysterious work . . .

And as the puffs of wind charged with big rain drops swirled faster about him, and the spread of grey clouds lengthened above him, there slowly rose around the conscript of Leon, on sentry duty before Casbah, stone houses of Brittany. A noise of bells ringing which, in a moment of calm, mounted from the Lower Town, from the French quarter, sounded through all his being, deeply. He remembered that it was Christmas Eve, the night made holy by the birth of a God.

And childish things came back again, in memory; things so sweet that they made him want to cry. Oh, the house of his father, the blaze of furze on the hearth, and the 'flip' – that punch of Arvos, so joyously drunk – and the golden chestnuts whose shells popped! It was as if he saw a veritable vision. The kitchen clock strikes eleven from the top of its wooden case; bustle stirs all the farm; everyone is soon indoors – all except the cattle who, this one night (they say) talk among themselves, in man's language, of the child newborn in the Galilean stable. It is a black night, in spite of the stars; one feels his way across the muddy roads, for the tradition of snow-white Christmases is dead; the seasons have changed their habits, like us men. In the cemetery there is a stirring among the tombs of the ancestors; the church doors, wide open, make luminous bays whence escapes the veiled melody of the chant of women. And in the chorus of voices the loved voice dominates – that which the Leonard of Casbah recognises among all the rest: yours, O Glaudinaïk of Mezoubrân, who doubtless think not of Africa as you chant those Latin verses . . .

His dream took on an intensity of actual life: he was playing himself into it with an infinitely delicious sadness when they came to relieve him of his post.

He had an hour before him, before evening roll call. How willingly he would have run to the cathedral, had it not been so far! He had to content himself with pursuing his meditative stroll through the alleyways swarming with Arabs. Dusk had abruptly fallen; the sky seemed an immense frozen bowl, pricked with glittering points; the caravan of clouds had disappeared.

Suddenly, as he came to a high and mournful facade, there sounded in his ears a faint, dragging music, a sort of monotonous murmur of prayer or lamentation. A narrow porch yawned in the shadow; he entered in.

III

A vast hall, dimly lighted; thick carpets spread upon the floor deadened all footfalls.

About pillars, towards the back, green flags hung from staffs, like the standards which deck the walls of chapels in Brittany on pardon day.

Vague crouching forms, draped in clothes of white, grey or blue, lay in a silent immobility. From time to time, however, a name escaped from their lips. This ran like a shiver of wind on a calm sea. One made out only one word, always the same:

'Allah! Allah!'

Then, and then only, did the veteran of San Thégonnek realise that he was in an Arab sanctuary, in a mosque, and that these folk on their knees were worshipping . . .

His brother, the priest, interrupted his story at this point:

'You should have gone out, Yvik; you should have gone out that very moment.'

'Why, no!' he continued. 'I stayed. I will even add, to be frank, that I didn't have one thought of beating it!'

Quite the reverse. An irresistible desire seized him, him, the Christian, to join his prayer to that of these miscreants.

He knelt behind their close ranks, and in the house of Mohammed he began, in the midst of all these Muslim orations, to recite his Catholic Pater Noster – in Breton.

The voice of the mufti, at the end of the nave, recited the slow melody of the Koran. Naively, without thinking of evil, he let himself go, his eyes half closed, and listened to the buzzing of the shrill voice; a bit quavery, yet with sweet modulations. And it brought back to him, try though he did to check the sacrilege of the comparison – yes, it brought back to him the old curate of his parish, and the low mass said in the Breton church, and the faint responses of the choir boy on the steps of the main altar.

Was it not, then, truly, at some Christmas Mass that he assisted? Wasn't he on the point of discovering somewhere, in one of the dim corners of the mosque, that simple cradle at which his sisters had lately been working, as the day of days drew near? He almost imagined he saw it there, near the mufti's pulpit: the roof of green boughs with flakes of cotton wool make-believe snow, the waxen Jesus on a bed of clean straw, the grave-faced Saint Joseph, the darling Virgin, and the welcoming nozzles of the animals. Nothing troubled the illusion; they even seemed to fortify it, all those forms prostrate before him, showing just their backs. The white backs gave you the impression of hooded nuns, while those in darker dress might readily be taken for the old women of the

49

Saint-Thégonnek country, wrapped in the long cloaks that they use for mourning, and in cold seasons.

Who knows if she wasn't there; in the midst of this exotic world – his Glaudinaïk of Mezoubrân? He could have sworn that she was going to rise in another minute, when Mass was over, and pass out with him, slender and exquisite, blushing faintly under her lace coif, the coif of the maids of Quimerch with spread wings. Now they would follow the muddy roads, bestriding the puddles with the hearty laughter where love sounds; and then they would sit down together in the farmhouse kitchen, for the Christmas Eve supper, an exquisite wake it would be, this feast in honour of the Jesus: greeted, as He came into the world, by shepherdfolk . . .

But Glaudinaïk did not arise; it was Arabs who crossed the threshold before him, contemplating him with keen eyes that looked daggers. Outside, it was the same immense sky like a frozen bowl; but, instead of there being white squalls as before, there blew the biting norther, cutting the face. And he felt that it was far away, the warmth that rides on the wind-wings of Brittany, even in heart of winter.

He climbed again towards the barracks, toward the quarters where his messmates were chaffing one another: his head empty and hollow-seeming – sick of soul.

'Come!' he said, in closing. 'To speak like my brother the abbot, perhaps it wasn't any too orthodox, but I shall remember all my life that midnight mass!' Then, turning towards his young wife seated on the bed bench, at the edge of the hearth, near the servants:

'In any case, Glaudinaïk, I never thought of you – even in the Khroumire country, where one sees Death's face – with more fervour!'

The soldier was silent. In the great hush you heard only the ticktock of the clock, and the song of the agonising yule log.

1897

THE WOODEN SHOES OF
LITTLE WOLFF

François Coppée

Once upon a time – so long ago that the world has for-gotten the date – in a city of the North of Europe – the name of which is so hard to pronounce that no one remembers it – there was a little boy, just seven years old, whose name was Wolff. He was an orphan and lived with his aunt, a hard-hearted, avaricious old woman, who never kissed him but once a year, on New Year's Day; and who sighed with regret every time she gave him a bowlful of soup.

The poor little boy was so sweet-tempered that he loved the old woman in spite of her bad treatment, but he could not look without trembling at the wart, decorated with four grey hairs, which grew on the end of her nose.

As Wolff's aunt was known to have a house of her own and a woollen stocking full of gold, she did not dare to send her nephew to the school for the poor. But she wrangled so that the schoolmaster of the rich boys' school was forced to lower his price and admit little Wolff among his pupils. The bad schoolmaster was vexed to have a boy so meanly clad and who paid so little, and he punished little Wolff severely without cause, ridiculed him, and even incited against him his comrades, who were the sons of rich citizens. They made the orphan their drudge and mocked at him so much that the little boy was as miserable as the stones in the street, and hid himself away in corners to cry when the Christmas season came.

On the eve of the great day the schoolmaster was to take all his pupils to the Midnight Mass, and then to conduct them home again to their parents' houses.

Now, as the winter was very severe, and a quantity of snow had fallen within the past few days, the boys came to the place of meeting warmly wrapped up, with fur-lined caps drawn down over their ears, padded jackets, gloves and knitted mittens, and good strong shoes with thick soles. Only little Wolff presented himself shivering in his thin everyday clothes, and wearing on his feet socks and wooden shoes.

His naughty comrades tried to annoy him in every possible way, but the orphan was so busy warming his hands by blowing on them, and was suffering so much from chilblains, that he paid no heed to the taunts of the others. Then the band of boys, marching two by two, started for the parish church.

It was comfortable inside the church, which was brilliant with lighted tapers. And the pupils, made lively by the gentle warmth, the sound of the organ, and the singing of the choir, began to chatter in low tones. They boasted of the midnight treats awaiting them at home. The son of the mayor had seen, before leaving the house, a monstrous goose larded with truffles so that it looked like a black-spotted leopard. Another boy told of the fir tree waiting for him, on the branches of which hung oranges, sugarplums, and punchinellos. Then they talked about what the Christ Child would bring them, or what he would leave in their shoes which they would certainly be careful to place before the fire when they went to bed. And the eyes of the little rogues, lively as a crowd of mice, sparkled with delight as they thought of the many gifts they would find on waking: the pink bags of burned almonds, the bonbons, lead soldiers standing in rows, menageries, and magnificent jumping jacks, dressed in purple and gold.

Little Wolff, alas, knew well that his miserly old aunt would send him to bed without any supper; but as he had been good and industrious all the year, he trusted that the Christ Child would not forget him, so he meant that night to set his wooden shoes on the hearth.

The Midnight Mass was ended. The worshippers hurried

away, anxious to enjoy the treats awaiting them in their homes. The band of pupils, two by two, following the schoolmaster, passed out of the church.

Now, under the porch, seated on a stone bench, in the shadow of an arched niche, was a child asleep – a little child dressed in a white garment and with bare feet exposed to the cold. He was not a beggar, for his dress was clean and new; beside him upon the ground, tied in a cloth, were the tools of a carpenter's apprentice.

Under the light of the stars, his face, with its closed eyes, shone with an expression of divine sweetness, and his soft, curling blond hair seemed to form an aureole of light about his forehead. But his tender feet, blue with the cold on this cruel night of December, were pitiful to see!

The pupils so warmly clad and shod passed with indifference before the unknown child. Some, the sons of the greatest men in the city, cast looks of scorn on the barefooted one. But little Wolff, coming last out of the church, stopped, deeply moved before the beautiful, sleeping child.

'Alas!' said the orphan to himself, 'how dreadful! This poor little one goes without stockings in weather so cold! And, what is worse, he has no shoe to leave beside him while he sleeps, so that the Christ Child may place something in it to comfort him in all his misery.'

And carried away by his tender heart, little Wolff drew off

the wooden shoe from his right foot, placed it before the sleeping child, and as best as he was able, now hopping, now limping, and wetting his sock in the snow, he returned to his aunt.

'You good-for-nothing!' cried the old woman, full of rage as she saw that one of his shoes was gone. 'What have you done with your shoe, little beggar?'

Little Wolff did not know how to lie, and, though shivering with terror as he saw the grey hairs on the end of her nose stand upright, he tried, stammering, to tell his adventure.

But the old miser burst into frightful laughter. 'Ah! the sweet young master takes off his shoe for a beggar! Ah! Master spoils a pair of shoes for a barefoot! This is something new, indeed! Ah! Well, since things are so, I will place the shoe that is left in the fireplace, and tonight the Christ Child will put in a rod to whip you when you wake. And tomorrow you shall have nothing to eat but water and dry bread, and we shall see if the next time you will give away your shoe to the first vagabond that comes along.'

And saying this the wicked woman gave him a box on each ear, and made him climb to his wretched room in the loft. There the heartbroken little one lay down in the darkness, and, drenching his pillow with tears, fell asleep.

But in the morning, when the old woman, awakened by the cold and shaken by her cough, descended to the kitchen – oh! Wonder of wonders!

She saw the great fireplace filled with bright toys, magnificent boxes of sugarplums, riches of all sorts, and in front of all this treasure, the wooden shoe which her nephew had given to the vagabond, standing beside the other shoe which she herself had placed there the night before, intending to put in it a handful of switches.

And as little Wolff, who had come running at the cries of his aunt, stood in speechless delight before all the splendid Christmas gifts, there came great shouts of laughter from the street.

The old woman and the little boy went out to learn what it was all about, and saw the gossips gathered around the public fountain. What could have happened? Oh, a most amusing and extraordinary thing! The children of all the rich men of the city, whose parents wished to surprise them with the most beautiful gifts, had found nothing but switches in their shoes!

Then the old woman and little Wolff remembered with alarm all the riches that were in their own fireplace, but just then they saw the pastor of the parish church arriving with his face full of perplexity.

Above the bench near the church door, in the very spot where the night before a child, dressed in white, with bare feet exposed to the great cold, had rested his sleeping head, the pastor had seen a golden circle wrought into the old stones. Then all the people knew that the beautiful, sleeping child, beside whom had lain the carpenter's tools, was the Christ Child himself, and that he had rewarded the faith and charity of little Wolff.

1889

CHRISTMAS

CHRISTMAS EVE

Guy de Maupassant

'**A** Christmas Eve supper! No, never again,' said Henri Templier, in a furious tone, as if someone had suggested his participation in some crime. The others laughed and said: 'Why do you fly into a rage?'

'Because a Christmas Eve supper played me the dirtiest trick in the world, and ever since I have felt an insurmountable horror for that night of imbecile gaiety.'

'Tell us about it!'

'You want to know what it was? Very well, then; just listen:

'You remember how cold it was two years ago at Christmas; cold enough to kill people in the streets. The Seine was covered with ice; the pavements froze one's feet through the soles of one's boots, and the whole world seemed to be about to come to an end.

'I had a big piece to work on, and so I refused every invitation to supper, as I preferred to spend the night at my writing table. I dined alone and then began to work. But about ten o'clock I grew restless at the thought of the gay and busy life all over Paris, at the noise in the streets which reached me in spite of everything, at the sound of my neighbours' preparations for supper, which I heard through the walls. I hardly knew any longer what I was doing; I wrote nonsense, and at last came to the conclusion that I had better give up all hope of producing any good work that night.

'I walked up and down my room; I sat down and got up again. I was certainly under the mysterious influence of the merriment outside, and I resigned myself to it. I rang for my servant and said to her:

'"Angela, go and get a good supper for two; some oysters, a cold partridge, some crayfish, ham, and some cakes. Put out two bottles of champagne, lay the cloth, and go to bed."

'She obeyed in some surprise, and when all was ready I put on my greatcoat and went out. A great question was to be solved: Whom was I going to bring in to supper? My female friends had all been invited elsewhere, and if I had wished to invite one, I ought to have seen about it beforehand, so, thinking that I would do a good action, I said to myself:

'"Paris is full of poor and pretty girls who will have nothing on their table tonight, and who are on the lookout for some generous fellow. I will act the part of Providence to one of them this evening; and I will find one if I have to go into every pleasure resort and have to question them and hunt till I find one to my choice." And I started off on my search.

'I certainly found many poor girls who were on the lookout for some adventure, but they were ugly enough to give any man a fit of indigestion, or thin enough to freeze on the spot if they had stood still. You all know that I have a weakness for stout women; the more embonpoint they have, the better I like them, and a female colossus would drive me out of my senses with delight.

'Suddenly, opposite the Théâtre des Variétés, I saw a profile to my liking. A good head and a full figure. I was charmed, and said "By Jove! What a fine girl!"

'It only remained for me to see her face. A woman's face is the dessert, while the rest is . . . the roast.

'I hastened on and overtook her, and she turned around suddenly under a gas lamp. She was charming, quite young, dark, with large black eyes, and I immediately invited her to supper. She accepted without any hesitation, and a quarter of an hour later we were sitting at supper in my lodgings. "Oh, how comfortable it is here!" she said as she came in, and she looked about her with evident satisfaction at having found a supper and a room on that bitter night. She was superb, so beautiful that she astonished me, and her figure fairly captivated me.

'She took off her cloak and hat, sat down, and began to eat, but she seemed in low spirits, and sometimes her pale face twitched as if she were suffering from some hidden sorrow.

'"Have you anything troubling you?" I asked her.

'"Bah! Don't let us think of troubles!"

'And she began to drink. She emptied her champagne glass at a draught, filled it again, and emptied it again, without stopping, and soon colour came into her cheeks, and she began to laugh.

'I adored her already, kissed her continually, and discovered that she was neither stupid, nor common, nor coarse as some ordinary girls are. I asked her for some details of her life, but she replied:

'"My little fellow, that is no business of yours!" Alas, an hour later . . .

'At last it was time to go to bed, and while I was clearing the table, which had been laid in front of the fire, she undressed herself quickly, and got in. My neighbours were making a terrible din, singing and laughing like lunatics, and so I said to myself:

'"I was quite right to go out and bring in this girl; I should never have been able to do any work."

'At that moment, however, a deep groan made me look around, and I said, "What is the matter with you, my dear?"

'She did not reply, but continued to utter painful sighs, as if she were suffering horribly, and I continued:

'"Do you feel ill?" And suddenly she uttered a cry, a heart-rending cry, and I rushed up to the bed, with a candle in my hand.

'Her face was distorted with pain, and she was wringing her hands, panting and uttering long, deep groans, which sounded like a rattle in the throat, and which are so painful to hear, and I asked her in consternation:

'"What is the matter with you? Do tell me what is the matter."

'"Oh! my stomach! my stomach!" she said. I pulled up the bedclothes, and I saw . . . My friends, she was in labour.

'Then I lost my head, and I ran and knocked at the wall with my fists, shouting: "Help! Help!"

'My door was opened almost immediately, and a crowd of people came in, men in evening dress, women in low necks, harlequins, Turks, musketeers, and this inroad startled me so that I could not explain myself, and they, who had thought that some accident had happened, or that a crime had been committed, could not understand what was the matter. At last, however, I managed to say:

'"This . . . this . . . woman . . . is giving birth."

'Then they looked at her and gave their opinion, and a friar, especially, declared that he knew all about it, and wished to assist nature, but as they were all as drunk as pigs, I was afraid that they would kill her, and I rushed downstairs without my hat, to fetch an old doctor who lived in the next street. When I came back with him the whole house was up; the gas on the stairs had been relighted, the lodgers from every floor were in my room, while four boatmen were finishing my champagne and lobsters.

'As soon as they saw me they raised a loud shout, and a milkmaid presented me with a horrible little wrinkled specimen of humanity, that was mewing like a cat, and said to me. "It's a girl."

'The doctor examined the woman, declared that she was in a dangerous state, as the event had occurred immediately after supper, and he took his leave, saying he would immediately send a sick nurse and a wet nurse, and an hour later the two women came, bringing all that was requisite with them.

'I spent the night in my armchair, too distracted to be able to think of the consequences, and almost as soon as it was light, the doctor came again, who found his patient very ill, and said to me:

'"Your wife, Monsieur . . ."

'"She is not my wife," I interrupted him.

'"Very well, then, your mistress; it does not matter to me."

'He told me what must be done for her, what her diet must be, and then wrote a prescription.

'What was I to do? Could I send the poor creature to the hospital? I should have been looked upon as a brute in the house and in all the neighbourhood, and so I kept her in my rooms, and she had my bed for six weeks.

'I sent the child to some peasants at Poissy to be taken care of, and she still costs me fifty francs a month, for as I had paid at first, I shall be obliged to go on paying as long as I live, and later on she will believe that I am her father. But to crown my misfortunes, when the girl had recovered . . . I found that she was in love with me, madly in love with me, the baggage!'

'Well?'

'Well, she had grown as thin as a homeless cat, and I turned the skeleton out of doors, but she watches for me in the streets, hides herself, so that she may see me pass, stops me in the evening when I go out, in order to kiss my hand, and, in fact, worries me enough to drive me mad; and that is why I never keep Christmas Eve now.'

1882

CHRISTMAS AT THE BOARDING SCHOOL

Dominique Fabre

This is an old story, a school story. I was in the third row and he was in the second, near the entrance. He had arrived in September and sometimes, when he wasn't busy listening in class, sharpening a pencil or writing an assignment, he looked around looking a bit lost, as if he'd just gotten off an airplane and didn't know where he was. Today, ages later, I think he would have struck me the same way. I surely wasn't alone in thinking this. He was a bit bigger than we were and definitely didn't dress the same. I couldn't say if his clothing cost more or less than ours. It didn't matter. Just by looking at him, the new guy, one could tell that it wasn't going to work out, that he wouldn't stay long among us. He was called Black Jo.

He had a godmother here who was a secretary in a large international organisation and she sometimes stopped by

unexpectedly when she had the time. She was a big, impos-
ing woman, she smiled with all her teeth; a woman like her
inspired confidence in life. She carried a little Chanel purse
and wore flat shoes, no doubt because she was very tall. Apart
from rare weekends when he went to her place, Black Jo led
the sad life of a somewhat abandoned child; his parents lived
far away in Senegal. They had to send him to France because
of 'events', he explained to us. From all over the world,
'events' make it necessary for kids to be kept safe, apart from
their family.

Black Jo knew the names of the players on the Africa Cup
teams, and the African players on French teams, who according to him, scored three times as many goals as the whites.
He had a fairly peremptory tone when he talked about soccer
scores, or strategy, and, while I had little interest in the game
and carefully avoided the ball, I remember that he would
often score goals. But he was ridiculed. He fervently main-
tained that Africans were the original inventors of the
bicycle, others contradicted him, and they almost came to
blows about the bike story. The wheels were wooden, without a chain, but they rolled just fine. The others didn't accept
his view: one more reason for the loneliness of Black Jo,
when his godmother couldn't have him come for the weekend. Black Jo was of mixed race; he had light skin, he had
freckles. He struggled in class. Believing it was the right

thing, the teachers seated him next to the kid from Marti-
nique, the pretentious son of a doctor. They didn't get along.

Other students sometimes had to spend the weekend at
the boarding school. Langinieux was among them; he asked
to stay since his parents didn't get along and he preferred to
avoid them. Sometimes, there were other students who were
kept back because of serious violations of the rules. Black Jo
had to spend some weekends entirely alone, when even Cal-
laghan, an English student far from his country, went to *his*
godmother's. These godmothers. I went home every weekend but mother sent me to my godmother as well, so as to get
rid of me. Sometimes I thought about Black Jo alone in the
boarding school. It wasn't fun for him.

On Friday evenings the students, looking forward to wild
weekends, put on their own clothes and packed their bags to
take the express train. Joseph watched all this activity without
any obvious sadness or bitterness. They went away in a group,
beyond the fence and shouting, waving, passing through the
second gate under the relieved watch of the teachers, because
they too were, after all, prisoners here. Black Jo had the dormitory to himself. He could go into the common room, to
which he had the key for the weekend, and where there was a
television in a cabinet; that was to watch soccer or rugby
matches, and in the spring the French Open or Wimbledon.
He had keys to the infirmary. He occasionally suffered from

migraines, and he never had to worry about getting permission to lie down, with perhaps a dose of aspirin or just a bit of nonmedical relief accorded to him by the nurse, a young pale woman with very light eyes devoid of sparkle, who wore stone-washed jeans. When she arrived each morning, we saw her cross the courtyard looking a bit lost, weary, considering all this terrain around her as still foreign, as if she were sizing it up. Maryse Gentil. Her walk across the courtyard is one of the most vivid memories I've retained from those years.

Since his arrival Black Jo had spent several weekends roaming around the big school to discover the different spots; the cafeteria, the large industrial kitchen and the athletic facilities, the building reserved for priests, a few of whom taught here and others who'd returned from missions to Africa, congregations where the school distributed funds for families. It involved raising money and tax reductions were given to the largest donors. There was the library, where Joseph often went because in the end he found his classmates idiotic, devoid of curiosity. They didn't understand that the world extended beyond the tip of their nose, the address of the rich kid's vacation house or summer camp for the others . . . he went to get his meal tray at the guardians' lodge; they lived in a small two-storey house.

Langinieux was one of the only ones who came to get news from Jo on Monday, a little after the nurse had crossed the courtyard on her way to the infirmary or while Joseph was waiting for her return or dreaming of his family in Senegal, waiting for the time to pass and expecting that we classmates would continue to laugh in disbelief upon learning about all that the Africans discovered, well before the little French who ran like goats and who had red ears during the math tests. What surprised us, apart from the stories about Senegal, was his faith in God's power; he volunteered to be a choirboy and got up for vigils. The vigils were a weird feature of the boarding school; there were hours of prayer during the night, since to carry away the sins of the world was no small matter and required a kind of marathon. For Joseph God was absolutely present in life, which bothered others who were more preoccupied by their grade point averages, sports scores or how to sneak into the nearby girls boarding school, playing the fox in the henhouse, not even in your dreams!

On Monday, I was coming back from the small suburban town where I had been bored all Sunday. I had hardly gone any farther than the Asnières station in one direction or the Tricycle Cinema in the other where I didn't go often. Jo never asked what we did over the weekend, it was a painful question for him. On Monday he chattered non-stop, as if he needed to empty himself of all the words he'd kept in for two days, often looking up at the sky. He described the clouds of his homeland, much more extraordinary than the tiny masses found in France. When he too had spent the weekend elsewhere, at his godmother's, having had a meal surrounded by her lovers, friends, neighbours, indeterminate relatives talking in several languages, including French, it took him a week to reacclimatise, to discover as if for the first time the grey buildings of the school and the athletic facilities that weren't a minor selling point of the institution. There he is again sitting in the second row, off to the side. It was now winter and Jo had made up his mind about this country, this school. Sometimes he looked out the windows to where the Seine flowed, about a mile in the distance. From there, he'd have had to ask the way to Orly Airport. Jo wore skimpy shirts and sandals; classmates gave him a sweater, shoes, so that he wouldn't drop dead from the cold. He talked a bit more about the wonders of his country, the lions, tigers, the shape of the clouds, of all the hours playing soccer on the beach. He showed his friends a picture of his house, surrounded by a white wooden fence. As for his clothes, the priests at the school had noticed them; the headmaster, who we were afraid of, said to him, you don't have any warm clothes, Joseph? Black Jo spent the evening in the common room, sitting on the radiator in his underpants, waiting for a classmate willing to be beaten at chequers because Africans are better

74

than we are at that game. Everyone told him he had to cover up now, this wasn't the Africa of his childhood, the place where according to him his parents still lived in a house surrounded by a white fence. France isn't my country, Black Jo would say, it's awful to live here. The teachers are mean to those who don't succeed and the French are selfish, that's what he thought, sitting there on the radiator in the common room.

Joseph had been playing chequers since he was very little; he learned by watching grown-ups at the market while his mother went shopping. We taught him to play cards. We didn't have the same games here as down there; here we were beaten on the back of the hand, and sometimes the students ended up brawling. I recall Joseph with his fists clenched close to his body, his tears spilling out against his long eyelashes and how he began to tremble. The mocking students didn't attack him directly, though. He said come on, I'm ready for you, to the boy who was after him, who did well not to go there. In any case, I recall from this dispute that the teacher in charge interrupted with an angry gesture, handing a tissue to Joseph, and then I found myself in the bed next to Black Jo, taking the place of the boy who used to sleep there, who called him a nigger and a faggot. Something must have happened since the next week he had new clothes, almost like ours, corduroy pants and a white long-sleeved shirt, but his outfits all had

labels and were decorated with a print that evoked Africa . . .
I suppose they had a certain appeal. He arranged them neatly
folded on the iron chair next to his bed.

He had truly been transplanted here. He had a kind of
patience, each evening I saw him pray with extraordinary
concentration. In Africa, he explained to us, people went to
mass, not just old women like in France, but also young
people like us and children. Then when he had finished he
opened the drawer of his night table and inspected his treasures, the letters from his parents; he never spoke about them
but with me, Langinieux and a few others he mentioned his
godmother, the walks they took together, the museums, the
friends to whose houses he accompanied her. She didn't find
it the least bit embarrassing to take him, the little light-
skinned African from Senegal who had no hope of returning
there for a long time, serious but somewhat lost in his school-
ing, to an evening of dancing. Once he picked up the
handkerchief that fell out of a man's vest and brought it back,
a shiny piece of cloth he often fingered and kept as a treasure
in the drawer of his night table, similar to fifty others in the
dormitory. He also kept photos, his mother in traditional
garb seemed very young in comparison to parents here; his
father, about whom he never spoke, photographed near the
Senegal River. He spoke to me several times about the
Senegal River, it was much more than a river for him.

When the lights were turned off, he had the habit of closing his eyes as if for a yoga exercise or as if he wanted to stay awake to continue a conversation or to whisper in the middle of the night. One time, however, one of the idiots who couldn't stand Black Jo went to open up his drawer and extract his treasures; I didn't dare to alert him for fear of retaliation. But Jo sensed something and once he'd opened his eyes, under his long lashes, he threw himself on the boy and if the teacher hadn't arrived in time he surely would have strangled him. As it was nighttime, the classmates didn't talk about the incident; Joseph inspected all the objects from his drawer and afterwards he kept an eye on every other bed until the sobbing student he'd almost strangled had closed his eyes again. He didn't reply to my 'good night'. We used to wish each other good night and to keep any eye out for each other at school; I was a kind of support, a pal to Black Jo, the mixed race African with freckles.

Things got worse for him from that night on. He was forced to stay in on a weekend when he'd been invited by his beautiful godmother from the international development organisation. A few of us came to his defence and explained what had happened. He was only defending his territory. The dean of students just shook his head without replying. Since we insisted, he ended up saying he would make us stay the next weekend too; the crazier it got the more we laughed.

We didn't win but it helped bring us closer to Black Jo. After free time he wanted to go out with us to smoke a cigarette. He was homesick, he missed Africa in general and even if we tried to persuade him that it was worth giving it a try here, bit by bit Langinieux and I began to hope that he would tell us his stories about the wooden bicycle, animal races, canoeing up the Senegal River, without really being able to change things. To fight off loneliness Black Jo enveloped himself in his memories, while waiting for the end of classes, between two weekends at his godmother's who was his only reason to hang on, and the masses he participated in as a choirboy.

It started snowing early that year and he returned from the lodge once he saw the first snowflakes of his life. There must have been three or four of us behind the big building and the gym near the little house at the entrance. Jo was carrying a letter. Sometimes stamps covered half the envelope. He occasionally received blue aerograms and mail on letterhead. Look, snow! He couldn't resist reaching out for the flakes, holding his letter in the other hand. Soon, sticking out his tongue and waddling like a fool, he put the letter in his pocket to enjoy the snow. He didn't read it right away, he was no doubt waiting until he was by himself. In class Black Jo did his assignments carefully and when it was time to go to the dining hall he went towards the upper window of the classroom, the snow was still falling, there must have been already over an inch on the handball and basketball courts and on the asphalt in the courtyard.

The little year sevens had already gone out to make snow-balls or try to slide around; some students were talking about their upcoming vacation in Val d'Isère or Les Arcs. Jo took out his letter from underneath his pile of notebooks and went up towards the dormitory to get his hat and gloves, I'm sure that he hadn't read his letter yet at that point. He put it on his bed and took out his gloves from the wardrobe that we shared, Langinieux was with us, then we went back down, all excited . . . He stopped on the middle of the stairs to look out the window again. From the side of the Saint Cucufat Forest a sort of fog had descended and the snow accumu-lated, as if it had decided to stick around longer this year, and not just two or three days as it often did in Paris. Yes, of course! He'd already seen snow in Africa! The world's high-est mountains were also there, and even if we gradually got tired of such comparisons, we pointed out for him the Alps, the Andes and Mt Everest, but he didn't sulk like he had before. We went out together. He had forgotten something in the dormitory.

Okay, Joseph, we'll wait for you here. At the side of the yard there was nothing better to do than to smoke a cigarette while waiting. It was Thursday and the next evening, we'd take the train to go back to our families. There would be celebrations and gifts, we all took a puff from a shared cigarette. The kids from the younger section played in the courtyard. At age eleven you ended up in this place. They ran after one another, got into fights, and later at eighteen the big ones were full of hope for their lives and what it would be like when they left . . . We should have been in the dining hall but he still wasn't there. We all had the same fear at the same time. We went up to the dormitory, we're going to look for Joseph, Monsieur . . . He was at the window, standing still, looking out at the woods, his gaze directed farther than the gym or the pool for all the area residents, he was turned towards Paris, or perhaps towards the lost Africa of his parents.

Joseph, aren't you coming to eat? . . . What's the matter? We're waiting for you! He just shrugged his shoulders like a moody child, without turning, he still held the letter in his hand. He surely carried the weight of the world on his shoulders at that moment. We got closer to him. Snow flew in the courtyard and the wind blew it back but if it continued like that the powder would cover the handball court and gradually hide the coloured markings.

Bad news? Langi asked Jo, but he continued to look out the tall windows. Suddenly he crumpled up the letter in his hand and threw it into a ball. I bent down to take it. We glanced down, Langi and I. The fog was getting thicker around the little woods where people went running, with its stream still full, even at the end of year. Joseph finally told us he was coming down.

We'll wait for you if you want.

Yes, we'll wait, Langi repeated. I went to put his crumpled letter on the night table. When he turned towards us after he said he was going to join us, without wanting to we looked at the night table . . . He would not be going back to Senegal for Christmas, although his father had promised him that he could; he looked as if he was struggling to keep himself from howling. He spoke in a dull voice. This wasn't home here, he wanted to go back to Africa, he didn't want to study among whites . . . Langi put his arm around his shoulders. Black Jo shook his head as he pulled away. We heard a noise.

What are you doing here? the tadpole asked us. He was an old priest known only by his nickname, we called him the tadpole because of his wrinkly eyes and his fat jowls atop a gaunt neck.

I'm looking for my hat, Jo replied, adding a hint of the accent he had three months ago when he got angry over our incredulity about all the inventions we didn't know had come from down there, where his parents lived and who had more or less abandoned him, in our view. He put the letter in his drawer. He had a few others but this one he put on top without the envelope. He also had an open package of cookies his godmother had given him last weekend at her place.

What are you going to do then for Christmas? we asked him while eating the cookies. He shrugged his shoulders.

You think it's going to snow for long?

Who knows? The snow never lasts long in Paris.

We're not gonna let you down, Langinieux said to him. It will get better some day, Jo, you'll see.

It really was a special Christmas. There was a lot of snow, it swirled on the asphalt, the wind blew it to the side towards the low wall where we sat whenever we could. We smoked cigarettes there and sometimes set off firecrackers; Joseph never sat there with us but sometimes when he felt like it he walked on the edge of everything that had a rim, a summit, he climbed trees. He even won a contest against a guy named Descoubes, a jock with Greek parents who were sort of hippies, I remember all those useless details. Langinieux had gone back to his usual buddies and they were trying to run COBOL computer programs, that was all new then. He watched Black Jo, who didn't seem too upset, except when he tried to climb up a basketball board, imitating monkeys, because he got angry at guys who made fun of him. It would be simpler not to live, sometimes. The snow had slowed and settled down, it was almost dry, it seemed. At the next recess Joseph went up to the dormitory, we watched him go up the stairs. He climbed them two at a time bending forwards, perhaps he wanted to reread his letter? Joseph stayed up there a long time. Another guy named Martinet came down, he crossed paths with Jo but he didn't say anything to him . . . he always wandered around in white trousers and let his bracelet dangle at the end of his wrist, he wore rings on all his fingers and carried a switchblade. Black Jo? Yes, my dears. He had a letter in his hands. He seemed upset. Just two more days and we're out of here.

We went back up to see him. We weren't sure he'd be there but he was. He held the letter against his heart and then changed his mind, he held it out so we could read it. The old sorrows of childhood last a lifetime. His parents couldn't let him go to Paris because of 'events', they were sorry but . . . He took it from us. Joseph had really long eyelashes. His prominent shoulder blades, that way he had of sometimes dancing in the aisle when he was fed up and needed to let off steam.

I don't want to stay here, he murmured. I can't take living here.

Sometimes, when he was thinking or when he needed to pass the time, he bit a lock of his hair, he pulled on it and twirled it around his finger for several minutes with his eyes closed.

Can't you call them on the phone?

Langinieux pulled out a cigarette from the pack and was

about to light it when Joseph held out his hand, he'd never tried to smoke before.

Can I have a taste, please?

He spat out the smoke while making a face. We'd expected something worse but it didn't happen. And it continued to snow. It was cold in the dormitory when we went to piss or brush our teeth. His mother had come with his godmother to accompany him at the start of the year. Here the only other black kid was the Martinican, and Jo was mixed race; there were quite a few Lebanese who stuck together and whose parents lived in the nicer areas of Paris. The next day, a Christmas meal was served prior to the actual holiday. On the dais, the teachers were served a bottle of red wine, they all looked cheerful. We'd practically forgotten the story of Black Jo, who wouldn't see his parents before the summer, if ever. It was a strange Christmas meal with chipped plates and Pyrex glasses, it was at that moment that Jo chose to break loose, in the hubbub of the dining room, the evening of the last day of classes.

The snow still hadn't had the last word, in the morning from the dormitory window one saw an immaculately beautiful surface. It took awhile for Langinieux and the others to notice his disappearance, had anybody seen him? When the bell rang to go back to class, his place was empty; the first teacher wasn't concerned, nor the second, but Langinieux began to find it odd, Jo's absence, where was he holed up? At recess the students remained quiet in the yard, and there was something like an accelerated film shot and we all looked up at the same moment, towards the big open window at the top of the building where Joseph was standing, oh damn, Jo! Joseph, be careful, cut the crap! I felt my heart pounding, or leaping, really leaping inside my chest and knocking against the bones. The teacher on recess duty whistled, Joseph stepped into the void, with his big worried smile. Langi and I ended up at the bottom of the stairs at the same time as Descoubes who ran faster than the others. He arrived first. We heard those below who were afraid or laughed because they didn't want to believe it. Descoubes took a breath with his arm on the large door. Black Jo danced on the ledge a good fifty feet above where all of us students were. The panicky teacher let out another whistle and got the students in a line so they perhaps would be shielded from the fall of the angel Black Jo, who was not going to see his parents again or the Senegal River, which caused him so much pain that he wanted to trash everything or put an end to his life.

Langi and I looked at each another. He came up behind Jo and Jo felt his presence, mine too. It was a difficult moment. At the side of his bed, he'd emptied his drawer of secrets, he had left his life in tatters and kept only sorrow. At one point,

Langiniuex found himself facing Jo at the window, the students were all screaming down below, they refused to get in a line. Langi took Jo by the shoulders. As soon as they got down, Descoubes closed the window. I tried to organise his letters and his things while Joseph was crying and couldn't stop. We stayed together. The principal arrived, out of breath since he wasn't used to climbing stairs. We had to recount what we'd witnessed and we thought we wouldn't see Jo again too soon. They didn't like that too much, the administration, it was very bad publicity. Just then I took it upon myself to hide his letters, his handkerchief and the souvenirs of his life from before in Africa. That didn't concern them, I thought.

They confined him to the infirmary. Maryse Gentil wasn't there. There was an attendant with him, he was sitting on the bench in the infirmary and the history teacher was there but was fed up with everything by that point. They turned on the radio. They listened to the news, to the hit parade where you were supposed to call in to the radio to vote for or against. Jo pulled his knees up under his chin. They were looking for his parents but then realised the problem when they opened his file. So they called his godmother in Paris. From the window we saw the large fir tree the younger kids had decorated with electric lights, red, blue and green near the entry gate, facing a bar called Chiquito. Sometimes the fragile snow cracked under our feet, but the footprints always turned around on themselves, they weren't leading any-where. The teacher indicated that we could sit with Jo while he waited for his godmother. He had nonetheless achieved his goal: he wasn't far from exhausting himself. The teacher put a drop of brandy in a glass of cocoa. We talked about the vacation and Joseph hallucinated whenever Langinieux talked about how he loved skiing, the cold . . . It was a strange last evening, one could say. The attendant gave us a moment to stretch our legs around nine in the evening. When we came back up, he smiled at us again and pulled out his flask.

Another drop, guys?

Sure boss, why not?

We heard the steps of high-heeled shoes on the stairs. Black Jo was dumbstruck and couldn't believe his ears. His godmother was there.

She carried her beautiful purse on a long gold chain, her high heels were a bit wet because she'd walked through the snow. When she arrived she smiled at us then she didn't stop staring at him.

Joseph, do you know some place where we can talk, the two of us?

She had a beautiful, deep voice. She also carried a plastic shopping bag. Well, we'll leave you, *au revoir Madame*! Yes, goodbye, she seemed nice in her big coat and the light-coloured pants of an African woman from a good neighbourhood. At the base of the building, Langi and I with the little that we'd drunk didn't feel the cold. The others weren't with us that evening. We had heard the noise in the lobby, when a soccer play didn't pan out, it was still one of those matches from the French Cup, the cup of all cups, or the European Cup. We went to watch from above, towards the little window on the side of the dormitory, where he went with his godmother, it was an urgent situation if she'd come like this at night. We saw clearly the decorated Christmas tree near the exit gate. She must have gone through there, if she'd parked outside. Or perhaps she didn't have a car and arrived by bus or taxi? We wanted to know if she had come to reproach him, or what?

After the match the students left the common room to go back to their own digs; we were about to leave here until next year. We went up the staircase silently, we wanted to go discretely past the little room where Jo and his godmother were talking. But she saw us, the door had remained open, I don't know if she did that on purpose. She gave us a big, calm smile, he was in front of her, his elbows on his knees, like one did often while listening to others. She gave us a sign to come join them, with her big nice smile. She held out her hand, when he told her our first names.

She had rushed there as soon as she got the phone call. So, you're okay? We told her yes, we're fine, and since there wasn't much more to say Langi suggested making tea. Do you want some? Jo remained silent. She nodded her head, yes, a tea, in this cold, *merci*! Not a problem. We'll be right back. We went to borrow the kettle from the teacher and asked for teabags, as long as he had his flask and you didn't forget to bring back the kettle all would be fine. The students had gone to bed, some of them had already closed their eyes. Don't stay up too long, understand? He'd already taken out his history books because he worked a good part of the night after lights out. About him I recall only that he had the blue eyes of a Norman countryman and long nose hair. We went down to get Pyrex cups in the common room. Outside, the snow didn't seem to be letting up. We'd brought everything. Your friends, here they are! She had a super beautiful smile, the godmother of Black Jo. We looked for the kettle stopper and while waiting for it to whistle we sat back down, we had even found some sugar. Jo watched all of this with a strange air, a bit dumbfounded. He'd been crying, I think.

From the shopping bag, she took out cakes that she'd wanted to give to him but since we were all drinking tea together . . . one could eat them now, no? She hadn't spoken much with us. She often looked out the high window where it seemed to snow more and more, as if it was never going to stop. Jo didn't speak anymore, he was perhaps very tired now, he ate the cakes she'd brought. The crumbs fell on his legs. After tea, I would have liked to go to sleep. I was used to sleeping at that hour, above all when it was snowing; there weren't big hopes for the next day and even Santa Claus's bag of gifts didn't seem likely to be full to the brim. He lifted up his head occasionally to smile and we saw the great effort he tried to make since he wanted to leave with her.

No, Joseph, you can't, not tonight. You know that well. It's not possible . . .

She reasoned with him gently, with a serious voice. Then he shook his head as if he was thrown back into an inner void, there where he was truly in pain because of the Christmas vacation. In two days, Joseph. She had a beautiful voice with which to say Joseph to Black Jo. She yawned and looked at her watch.

It's going to be okay, you're going to sleep?

Langi and I we left the two of them. We brought back the kettle. *Au revoir, et merci* . . . She gave us her hand.

Langi read a page of a book with a flashlight before closing it and lying on his stomach. I hadn't taken off either my shirt or my sweater, I was lying on my side. I was waiting for Black Jo. If he was in the next bed, would I have dreamed of lions and African bicycles without chains? It bothered us that he didn't have his parents here, but only far away in Africa near the Senegal River. When the dormitory supervisor had finished his rounds, he drew his curtain and I saw him as if in a shadow box theatre. His little table. His coat stand. His little shelf. His satchel. His life. My eyes stung when I saw at the end of corridor, he was going down the stairs with his godmother. Her purse hung at the top of her arm, he gave her his hand, as if the stairs were dangerous, but they weren't. He wanted to get close to her, she didn't let him. The shadow box theatre of the supervisor, the flask on the small table. To your health, my friend, I told myself.

Joseph and his godmother at the edge of the field were looking towards the fence.

What terrible weather this country has, my Lord! she said. I hope I don't slip on the road!

She held the two sides of her coat tightly in her hand. If he lived with her in Paris he wouldn't take up too much room and wouldn't cost her much money . . . Two days, Joseph, that's not long . . . go, go back. He held her in his arms and I saw how much pleasure that gave him, she took his arms so she could free herself, laughing.

Stop, let me go now.

After passing the last lamp post of the field she looked back but couldn't see Black Jo, he was crouching down a bit farther in the courtyard. He held his hands out towards the flakes, but didn't catch any. They flew around him under the halo of the light. He could have stayed hours here, and died, I told myself. Well, okay. I came out from underneath the stairs.

Jo, you coming, let's go up?

I have to piss, don't you?

We looked towards the dormitory windows and it was all clear. We went towards the tree by the fence where his godmother had walked past, before driving off in her little Datsun Cherry. It was a big, old fir. The winter did it good, one could say. The coloured lights shined brightly. I'd heard that you could cause a short circuit by pissing on the transformer, but apart from two or three sparks nothing happened. Joseph was completely numb now. He was probably hoping to find a place to live in Paris when school resumed in January. When he came of age, he would return to Dakar. His godmother would explain it to them. It was his Christmas present. That's what he told me as he placed his feet in the same tracks that we made on the way there; he didn't like snow too much, even if it was really beautiful, when no one has sullied it and it falls heavily for no reason.

2017

SALVETTE AND BERNADOU

Alphonse Daudet

I

It was Christmas Eve in a great Bavarian town. A joyous crowd pushed its way through the streets white with snow, in the confusion of the fog, the rumble of carriages, and the clamour of bells, towards the booths, stalls, and cook-shops in the open air. Great fir trees bedecked with dangling gewgaws were being carried about, grazing the ribbons and flowers of the booths and towering above the crowd like shadows of Thuringian forests, a breath of Nature in the artificial life of winter.

It is twilight. The lingering lights of sunset, sending a crimson glow through the fog, can still be seen from the gardens beyond the Residence; and in the town the very air is so full of animation and festivity that every light that blinks through a windowpane seems to be dangling from a Christmas tree. For this is not an ordinary Christmas. It is the year of our Lord 1870; and the birth of Christ is but an additional pretext for drinking the health of the illustrious von der Than, and celebrating the triumph of Bavarian warriors. Christmas! Christmas! The Jews of the lower town themselves have joined in the general merriment. Here comes old Augustus Cahn, hurrying around the corner of the café called The Bunch of Blue Grapes. There is an unusual light in his ferret eyes. His little bushy pigtail was never known to wriggle so merrily. Over his sleeve, worn shiny by the rope handles of his wallet, he carries an honest basket, quite full, covered with a brown linen napkin, from under which peep the neck of a bottle and a twig of holly.

What the deuce is the old usurer up to? Can he too be celebrating Christmas? Has he assembled his friends and family to drink to the *Vaterland*? Impossible. Everybody knows that old Cahn has no Fatherland but his money safe. Neither has he relatives nor friends; he has only creditors. His sons, or rather his partners, have been away for three months with the army. They are trading yonder behind the luggage vans of the *Landwehr*, selling brandy, buying clocks, ripping the knapsacks fallen by the wayside, and searching the pockets of the dead at night on the battlefield. Father

Cahn, too old to follow his children, has remained in Bavaria, where he is doing a flourishing business with the French prisoners. He hovers about the quarters, loans money on watches, buys epaulets, medals, and money orders. He ferrets his way through hospitals and ambulances, and creeps noiselessly to the bedside of the wounded, inquiring in his hideous jargon, 'Aff you zumting to zell?'

And now he is trotting along hurriedly with his basket on his arm, because the military hospital closes at five, and because two Frenchmen are waiting for him there, in that great gloomy building behind the iron grating of narrow windows, where Christmas finds nothing to cheer its vigil but the pale lamps that burn at the bedside of the dying.

II

These two Frenchmen are Salvette and Bernadou, two light infantry men, two Provençals from the same village, enlisted in the same battalion and wounded by the same shell. But Salvette has proved the hardier of the two; he is able now to get up and to take a few steps from his bed to the window. Bernadou, on the other hand, has no desire to recover. Behind the faded curtains of his hospital bed, he languishes and grows thinner day by day; and when he speaks of his home, he smiles that sad smile of invalids which contains more resignation than hope. He seems a little brighter today, however, as he recalls the celebration of Christmas, which in our beautiful land of Provence is like a bonfire lighted in the heart of winter. He thinks of the walk home after midnight Mass, of the bedecked and luminous churches, the dark and crowded village streets, then the long evening around the table, the three traditional torches, the aïoli, the dish of snails, the pretty ceremony of the *cacho fio*, the Yule log, which the grandfather parades through the house and sprinkles with mulled wine.

'Ah, my poor Salvette, what a dreary Christmas this will be! If we only had a few cents left, we could buy a little loaf of white bread and a bottle of light wine. It would be nice to sprinkle the Yule log with you once more before –' And his sunken eyes shine when he thinks of the wine and the white bread. But what is to be done? They have nothing left, the poor wretches, no watches, no money. True, Salvette has a money order for forty francs stored away in the lining of his vest. But that must be kept in reserve for the day of their release, or rather for the first halt at a French inn. It is sacred money, and cannot be touched. Still, poor Bernadou is so low, who can tell whether he will ever live through the journey home? And while it is still time, might it not be better to celebrate this Christmas together? Without saying a word of it to his comrade, Salvette rips his vest lining; and after a long struggle and a whispered discussion with Augustus Cahn, he slips into his hand this little scrap of stiff yellow paper smelling of powder and stained with blood, after which he assumes a look of deep mystery. He rubs his hands and laughs softly to himself as he glances over at Bernadou. As the darkness falls, he stands with his forehead against the windowpane, and stirs from his post only when he sees old Augustus Cahn turn the corner breathlessly, with a little basket on his arm.

III

The solemn midnight, ringing from all the steeples of the great city, falls lugubriously on the insomnia of the wounded. The hospital is silent, lighted only by the night lamps that swing from the ceiling. Gaunt shadows float over the beds and the bare walls with a perpetual swaying, which seems like the oppressed breathing of the people lying there. Every now and then there are dreams which talk aloud, or nightmares that moan; while vague murmurs of steps and voices, blended in the sonorous chill of the night, rise from the street like sounds issuing from the portals of a cathedral. They are fraught with impressions of pious haste, the mystery of a religious festival invading the hours of sleep and filling the darkness of the city with the soft glow of lanterns and the jewelled radiance of church windows.

'Are you asleep, Bernadou?'

On the little table by his friend's bed Salvette has laid a bottle of Lunel wine and a pretty round Christmas loaf with a twig of holly stuck in the top. The wounded man opens his eyes, dark and sunken with fever. In the uncertain light of the night lamps and the reflection of the long roofs, where the moon dazzles herself in the snow, this improvised Christmas supper strikes him as something fantastic.

'Come, wake up, countryman; let it not be said that two Provençals let Christmas go by without sprinkling it with a draught of wine.'

And Salvette raises him on his pillows with a mother's tenderness. He fills the glasses, cuts the bread. They drink and speak of Provence. Bernadou seems to be cheered by the reminiscences and the white wine. With that childishness which invalids seem to find again in the depths of their weakness he begs for a Provençal carol. His comrade is only too happy.

'What shall it be, "The Host" or "The Three Kings" or "Saint Joseph Told Me?"'

'No, I prefer "The Shepherds". That is the one we used to sing at home.'

'Very well, then. Here goes, "The Shepherds".'

And in a low voice, with his head under the bed curtains, Salvette begins to sing. At the last verse, when the shepherds have laid down their offering of fresh eggs and cheeses, and Saint Joseph speeds them with kind words,

'Shepherds.

Take your leave,' – poor Bernadou slips back and falls heavily on his pillow.

His comrade, who believes that he has gone to sleep again, shakes him by the arm and calls him; but the wounded man remains motionless, and the twig of holly lying beside him looks like the green palm that is laid on the couch of the dead. Salvette has understood. He is slightly tipsy with the celebration and the shock of his sorrow; and with a voice full of tears he sings out, filling the silent dormitory with the joyous refrain of Provence,

'Shepherds,

Take your leave.'

1873

A CHRISTMAS SUPPER
IN THE MARAIS

Alphonse Daudet

Majesté, a seltzer water manufacturer of the Marais, has just indulged in a little Christmas supper with a few friends from the Place Royale, and walks home humming. The clock at St Paul's strikes two.

'How late it is!' thinks the good man as he hurries along. But the pavement is slippery, the streets are dark, and then, in this devil of an old neighbourhood which belongs to the time when carriages were scarce, there are the greatest number of turns, corners, steps, and posts in front of the houses for the accommodation of horsemen, all of which are calculated to impede a man's progress, particularly when his legs are heavy and his sight somewhat blurred by the toasts of the Christmas supper. M. Majesté reaches his destination at last, however. He stops before a great doorway above which gleams in the moonlight the freshly gilded coat-of-arms, the recently retouched armorial bearings which he has converted into a trademark.

FORMER

HÔTEL DE NESMOND

MAJESTÉ, JR.,

SELTZER WATER MANUFACTURER

The old Nesmond coat-of-arms stands out, resplendent, on all the siphons of the factory, on all the memoranda and letterheads.

The doorway leads directly to the court – a large, sunny court which floods the narrow street with light even at noon, when the portals are thrown open. Far back in this court stands a great and ancient structure, blackened walls covered with lacework and embroideries of stone, bulging iron balconies, stone balconies with pilasters, great high windows crowned with pediments, and capitals rearing their heads along the upper storeys like so many little roofs within the roof, then above it all, set in the very slate, the mansard dormer windows, like the round mirrors of a boudoir, daintily framed with garlands. From the court to the first story rises a great stone stairway gnawed and worn green by the rains. A meagre vine dangles along the wall, lifeless and black like the rope that swings from the pulley in the attic; and the whole has an indescribable air of sad grandeur and decay.

This is the ancient *Hôtel* de Nesmond. In the broad light of day it has quite a different aspect. The words 'Office', 'Storage', 'Entrance to the work-rooms', in bright gilt letters, seem to rejuvenate the old walls and infuse a new life into them. The drays from the railroad shake the iron portals as they rumble through, and the clerks step out on the landing to receive the goods. The court is obstructed with cases, baskets, straw, wrappers, and packing cloth. One is conscious of being in a factory. But at night, in the death-like stillness, with the winter moon casting and tangling fantastic shadows through the confused intricacy of all these roofs, the old dwelling of the Nesmonds resumes its lordly air. The court of honour seems to expand; the wrought iron of the balconies looks like fine lace; the old stairway is full of shadows in the uncertain light, of mysterious recesses like those of a cathedral; there are empty niches and half concealed steps that suggest an altar.

On this particular night M. Majesté is deeply impressed with the grandeur of his dwelling. The echo of his own footsteps startles him as he crosses the great deserted court. The stairway seems even broader than usual, and peculiarly heavy to climb. But that is the Christmas supper, no doubt. At the first landing he stops to take a breath; he leans on one of the windowsills. So much for living in a historic mansion! M. Majesté is certainly not a poet, oh, no! and still as he gazes around him at this lordly old place, which seems to be sleeping so peacefully under its benumbed, snow-hooded roofs, as he looks down into this grand, aristocratic old court which the moon floods with a bluish light, weird fancies flash through his brain.

'Suppose the Nesmonds should take it into their heads to come back, eh?'

Just then there is a violent pull at the doorbell. The portal swings open instantly, so brusquely that it puts out the light of the lamp post in the court. From the shadow of the doorway come rustling sounds and confused whisperings. There seems to be a great crowd wrangling and jostling to get in. There are footmen, a multitude of footmen, coaches with glass panes glimmering in the moonlight, sedan chairs swaying lightly between two torches whose long flames writhe and twist in the draught of the doorway. In a second the court is crowded; but at the foot of the stairway the confusion ceases. People alight from the coaches, recognise one another, smile, bow, and make their way up the stairs, chatting softly as though they were quite familiar with the house. There is much rustling of silks and clanking of swords on the landing, and billows of white hair, heavy and dull with powder. Through the faint sound of the airy tread comes a thin, high quiver of voices and little peals of laughter that has lost its vibration. All these people seem old, very old – eyes that have lost their fire, slumbering jewels that have lost their light, antique brocades that shimmer with a subdued iridescence in the light of the torches, and above it all a thin mist of powder that rises at every courtesy from the white-puffed scaffoldings of these stately heads. In a moment the place seems to be haunted. Torches glitter from window to window and up and down the curving stairways; the very dormers in the mansard twinkle with joy and life. The whole mansion is ablaze with light, as though a great burst of sunset had set its windows aglow.

'Merciful saints! They will set the house on fire!' thinks M. Majesté, and having recovered from his stupor, he makes an effort to shake the numbness from his legs, and hurries down into the court, where the footmen have just lighted a great bonfire. M. Majesté goes up to them, speaks to them, but they do not answer. They stand there chatting among themselves softly, and not the faintest breath issues from their lips into the freezing shadow of the night. M. Majesté is somewhat put out. He is reassured, however, when he realises that this great fire with its long straight flames is a most peculiar fire, which emits no heat, which simply glows, but does not burn. The good man therefore sets his mind at rest, goes upstairs again, and makes his way into the storage.

These storage rooms on the first floor must have been grand reception halls in their day. Particles of tarnished gold still cling to the angles. Mythological frescoes circle about the ceilings, wind around the mirrors, hover above the doorways, vague and subdued, like bygone memories. Unfortunately there are no curtains or furniture anywhere, nothing but baskets, great cases filled with leaden-headed siphons, and the withered limb of an old lilac bush rising in black outline outside the window.

M. Majesté enters. He finds the rooms crowded and brilliantly illumined. He bows, but nobody seems to notice him. The women, in their satin wraps, lean on their cavaliers' arms and flirt with ceremonious, mincing graces. They promenade, chat, separate into groups. All these old marquises really seem quite at home. One little shade stops, all aquiver, before a painted pier glass, then she glances smilingly at a Diana that rises out of the woodwork, lithe and roseate, with a crescent on her brow.

'This is I! Think of it! And here I am!'

'Nesmond, come and see your crest!' and they laugh immoderately at the sight of the Nesmond coat-of-arms displayed on the wrappers above the name of Majesté, Jr.

'Ha, ha, ha! Majesté! There are some majesties left in France after all, then!'

And there is no end of merriment, of mincing coquetries.

Little trills of laughter rise like the notes of a flute in the air. Someone exclaims suddenly:

'Champagne! Champagne!'

'Nonsense!'

'Yes, indeed, champagne. Come, Countess, what say you to a little Christmas supper?'

They have mistaken M. Majesté's seltzer water for champagne. They naturally find it somewhat flat. But these poor little ghosts have such unsteady heads! The foam of the seltzer water somehow excites them and makes them feel like dancing. Minuets are immediately organised. Four rare violinists provided by Nesmond strike out with an old melody by Rameau, full of triplets, quaint and melancholy in its vivacity, and you should see the pretty little grandmothers turn slowly and bow gravely in time with the music.

Their very finery seems freshened and rejuvenated by the sound, and so do the waistcoats of cloth-of-gold, the brocaded coats and diamond-buckled shoes. The panels themselves seem to awake. The old mirror, scratched and dim, which has stood encased in the wall for over two hundred years, recognises them all, glows softly upon them, showing them their own images with a pale vagueness like a tender regret.

In the midst of all this elegance M. Majesté feels somewhat ill at ease. He is huddled in a corner, and looks on from behind a case of bottles. But gradually the day dawns.

Through the glass doors of the storage rooms one can see the court growing light, then the top of the windows, then all one side of the great parlour. Before the light of day the figures melt and disappear. The four little violinists alone are belated in a corner, and M. Majesté watches them evaporate as the daylight creeps upon them. In the court below he can just see the vague form of a sedan chair, a powdered head sprinkled with emeralds, and the last spark of a torch that a lackey has dropped on the pavement, and which blends with the sparks from the wheels of a dray, rumbling in noisily through the open portals.

1872

A MIRACLE

Guy de Maupassant

Doctor Bonenfant was searching his memory, saying, half aloud: 'A Christmas story – some remembrance of Christmas?'

Suddenly he cried: 'Yes, I have one, and a strange one too; it is a fantastic story. I have seen a miracle! Yes, ladies, a miracle, and on Christmas night.'

'It astonishes you to hear me speak thus, a man who believes scarcely anything. Nevertheless, I have seen a miracle! I have seen it, I tell you, seen, with my own eyes, that is what I call seeing. Was I very much surprised, you ask? Not at all; because if I do not believe from your viewpoint, I believe in faith, and I know that it can remove mountains. I could cite many examples, but I might make you indignant, and I should risk diminishing the effect of my story.

'In the first place, I must confess that if I have not been

convinced and converted by what I have seen, I have at least been strongly moved; and I am going to strive to tell it to you naively, as if I had the credulity of an Auvergnat.

'I was then a country doctor, living in the town of Rolleville, on the plains of Normandy. The winter that year was terrible. By the end of November the snow came after a week of heavy frosts. One could see from afar the great snow clouds coming from the north, and then the descent of the white flakes commenced. In one night the whole plain was in its winding sheet. Farms, isolated in their square incisures, behind their curtains of great trees powdered with hoar frost, seemed to sleep under the accumulation of this thick, light-coloured covering.

'No noise could reach this dead country. The crows alone in large flocks outlined long festoons in the sky, living their lives to no purpose, swooping down upon the livid fields and picking at the snow with their great beaks. There was nothing to be heard but the vague, continued whisper of this white powder as it persistently fell. This lasted for eight days and then stopped. The earth had on its back a mantle five feet in thickness. And during the next three weeks, a sky spread itself out over this smooth, white mass, hard and glistening with frost, which was clear as blue crystal by day, and at night all studded with stars, as if the hoar frost grew by their light.

'The plain, the hedges, the elms of the enclosures, all

seemed dead, killed by the cold. Neither man nor beast went out. Only the chimneys of the cottages, clothed in white linen, revealed concealed life by the fine threads of smoke which mounted straight into the frosty air. From time to time one heard the trees crack, as if their wooden limbs were breaking under the bark. And sometimes a great branch would detach itself and fall, the resistless cold petrifying the sap and breaking the fibres. Dwellings set here and there in fields seemed a hundred miles away from one another. One lived as he could. I alone endeavoured to go to my nearest clients, constantly exposing myself to the danger of remaining in some hole in the winding sheet of snow.

'I soon perceived that a mysterious terror had spread over the country. Such a plague, they thought, was not natural. They pretended that they heard voices at night, and sharp whistling and cries, as of someone passing. These cries and the whistles came, without doubt, from emigrant birds which travelled at twilight and flew in flocks towards the south. But it was impossible to make these frightened people listen to reason. Fear had taken possession of their minds, and they listened to every extraordinary event.

'The forge of Father Vatinel was situated at the end of the hamlet of Epivent, on the highway, now invisible and deserted. As the people needed bread, the blacksmith resolved to go to the village. He remained some hours chattering with the inhabitants of the six houses that formed the centre of the country, took his bread and his news and a little of the fear that had spread over the region and set out before night.

'Suddenly, in skirting a hedge, he believed he saw an egg on the snow; yes, an egg was lying there, all white like the rest of the world. He bent over it, and in fact it was an egg. Where did it come from? What hen could have gone out there and laid an egg in that spot? The smith was astonished; he could not comprehend it; but he picked it up and took it to his wife.

'"See, wife, here is an egg that I found on the way."

'The woman tossed her head, replying:

'"An egg on the way? And this kind of weather! You must be drunk, surely."

'"No, no, my lady, it surely was at the foot of the hedge, and not frozen but still warm. Take it; I put it in my bosom so that it wouldn't cool off. You shall have it for your dinner."

'The egg was soon shining in the saucepan where the soup was simmering, and the smith began to relate what he had heard around the country. The woman listened, pale with excitement.

'"Surely I have heard some whistling," said she, "but it seemed to come from the chimney."

'They sat down to table, ate their soup first and then, while the husband was spreading the butter on his bread, the woman took the egg and examined it with a suspicious eye. "And if there should be something in this egg," said she.

'"What, think you, would you like to have in it?"

'"I know very well."

'"Go ahead and eat it. Don't be a fool." She opened the egg. It was like all eggs, and very fresh. She started to eat it but hesitated, tasting, then leaving, then tasting it again. The husband said: "Well, how does it taste, that egg?"

'She did not answer, but finished swallowing it. Then, suddenly, she set her eyes on her husband, fixed, haggard, and excited, raised her arms, turned and twisted them, convulsed from head to foot, and rolled on the floor, sending forth horrible shrieks. All night she struggled in these frightful spasms, trembling with fright, deformed by hideous convulsions. The smith, unable to restrain her, was obliged to bind her. And she screamed without ceasing, with voice indefatigable:

'"I have it in my body! I have it in my body!"

'I was called the next day. I ordered all the sedatives known, but without effect. She was mad. Then, with incredible swiftness, in spite of the obstacle of deep snow, the news, the strange news ran from farm to farm: "The smith's wife is possessed!" And they came from all about, not daring to go into the house, to listen to the cries of the frightened woman, whose voice was so strong that one could scarcely believe it belonged to a human creature.

'The curate of the village was sent for. He was a simple old priest. He came in surplice, as if to administer comfort to the dying, and pronounced with extended hands some formulas of exorcism, while four men held the foaming, writhing woman on the bed. But the spirit was not driven out.

'Christmas came without any change in the weather. In the early morning the priest came for me.

'"I wish," said he, "to ask you to assist me tonight at service for this unfortunate woman. Perhaps God will work a miracle in her favour at the same hour that he was born of a woman."

'I replied: "I approve heartily, Monsieur l'Abbé, but if the spell is to be broken by ceremony (and there could be no more propitious time to start it) she can be saved without remedies."

'The old priest murmured: "You are not a believer, Doctor, but aid me, will you not?" I promised him my aid.

'The evening came, and then the night. The clock on the church was striking, throwing its plaintive voice across the vast extent of white, glistening snow. Some black figures were wending their way slowly in groups, drawn by the bronze call from the bell. The full moon shone with a dull, wan light at the edge of the horizon, rendering more visible the desolation of the fields. I had taken four robust men with me, and with them repaired to the forge.

'The Possessed One shouted continually, although bound to her bed. They had clothed her properly, in spite of her resistance, and now they brought her out. The church was full of people, illuminated but cold; the choir chanted their monotonous notes; the serpent hummed; the little bell of the acolyte tinkled, regulating the movements of the faithful.

'I had shut the woman and her guards into the kitchen of the parish house and awaited the moment that I believed favourable.

'I chose the time immediately following communion. All the peasants, men and women, had received their God, resolving to submit to the severity of His will. A great silence prevailed while the priest finished the divine mystery. Upon my order, the door opened and the four men brought in the mad woman.

'When she saw the lights, the crowd on their knees, the choir illuminated, and the gilded tabernacle, she struggled with such vigor that she almost escaped from us, and she gave forth cries so piercing that a shiver of fright ran through the church. All bowed their heads; some fled. She had no longer the form of a woman, her hands being distorted, her countenance drawn, her eyes protruding. They held her up until after the march of the choir, and then allowed her to squat on the floor.

'Finally, the priest arose; he waited. When there was a moment of quiet, he took in his hands a silver vessel with the bands of gold, upon which was the consecrated white wafer and, advancing some steps, extended both arms above his head and presented it to the frightened stare of the maniac. She continued to shout, but with eyes fixed upon the shining object. And the priest continued thus, motionless, as if he had been a statue.

'This lasted a long, long time. The woman seemed seized with fear, fascinated; she looked fixedly at the bright vessel, trembled violently but at intervals, and cried out incessantly, but with a less piercing voice.

'It happened that she could no longer lower her eyes; that they were riveted on the Host, that she could no longer groan, that her body became pliable and that she sank down exhausted. The crowd was prostrate, brows to earth.

'The Possessed One now lowered her eyelids quickly, then raised them again, as if powerless to endure the sight of her God. She was silent. And then I myself perceived that her eyes were closed. She slept the sleep of the somnambulist, the hypnotist – pardon! – conquered by the contemplation of the silver vessel with the bands of gold, overcome by the Christ victorious.

'They carried her out, inert, while the priest returned to the altar. The assistants, thrown into wonderment, intoned a

Te Deum. The smith's wife slept for the next four hours; then she awoke without any remembrance either of the possession or of the deliverance. This, ladies, is the miracle that I saw.'

Doctor Bonenfant remained silent for a moment, then he added, in a rather disagreeable voice:

'And I could never refuse to swear to it in writing.'

1882

I TAKE SUPPER WITH MY WIFE

Antoine Gustave Droz

It was Christmas Eve, and a devilishly cold night. The snow fell in great flakes, which the wind beat against the windowpanes. The distant chimes reached us, confused and faint through the heavy, cottony atmosphere. The passers-by, muffled in their cloaks, glided along hurriedly, brushing by the walls of the houses, bending their heads before the wind. Wrapped in my dressing gown, I smiled as I drummed on the windowpane, smiled at the passers-by, at the north wind and the snow, with the smile of a happy man who is in a warm room with his feet in a pair of flannel-lined slippers which sink into a thick, soft carpet.

My wife sat in a corner of the hearth with a piece of cloth before her which she cut and trimmed off; and every now and then she raised her eyes, which met mine. A new book lay on the mantelpiece awaiting me, and a log in the fireplace whistled as it spit out those little blue flames which tempt one to poke it.

'There is nothing so stupid as a man trudging along in the snow. Is there?' said I.

'Sh-h-h!' said my wife, laying down her scissors. Then she stroked her chin thoughtfully with her tapering pink fingers, slightly plump at the extremities, and looked over very carefully the pieces she had just cut out.

'I say that it is absurd to go out into the cold when it is so easy to stay at home by the fire.'

'Sh-h-h!'

'What the deuce are you doing that is so important?'

'I – I am cutting out a pair of suspenders for you,' and she resumed her task. Her hair was coiled a little higher than usual; and where I stood, behind her, I could just see, as she leaned over her work, the nape of her neck, white and velvety. Innumerable soft little locks curled there gracefully, and this pretty down reminded me of those ripe peaches into which we drive our teeth greedily. I leaned nearer to see and kissed my wife on the neck.

'Monsieur!' exclaimed Louise, turning suddenly around.

'Madame!' and we both burst into a laugh.

'Come, come, on Christmas Eve!'

'Monsieur apologises?'

'Madame complains?'

'Yes; Madame complains. Madame complains of your not being more moved, more thrilled by the spirit of Christmas.

The *ding-ding-dong* from the bells of Notre Dame awakens no emotion in you; and when the magic lantern went by under your very window, you were perfectly unmoved, utterly indifferent. I watched you attentively, though I pretended to work.'

'Unmoved? Indifferent? I? When the magic lantern went by! Ah, my dear! You judge me very severely, and really –'

'Yes, yes, laugh if you will. It is nevertheless true that the pretty memories of your childhood are lost.'

'Come, my pet, would you like me to stand my boots in the fireplace tonight before I go to bed? Would you like me to stop the magic lantern man and go and get him a sheet and a candle-end, as my mother used to do? I can almost see her as she handed him the sheet. "Be careful you don't tear it, now," she would say; and we all clapped our hands in the mysterious obscurity. I remember all those joys, dear; but, you see, so many things have happened since. Other pleasures have obliterated those.'

'Yes, I understand, the pleasures of your bachelorhood! Come, now, I am sure this is the first Christmas Eve that has ever found you by your own fireside, in your dressing gown and without a supper, because you always had supper; that goes without saying.'

'Why, I don't know –'

'Yes, yes, I wager you always had a supper.'

'Well, perhaps I did, once or twice, although I scarcely remember; I may have had supper with a few old friends. And what did it all amount to? Two pennies' worth of chestnuts and –'

'And a glass of sugar and water.'

'Well, just about. Oh, it was nothing much, I can assure you! It sounds great at a distance. We talked awhile, and then we went to bed.'

'And he says all that with the straightest face! You have never breathed a word of these simple pleasures to me.'

'But, my dear, what I tell you is the absolute truth. I remember once, however, at Ernest's, when I was in rather high spirits, we had a little music afterwards. Will you push me that log? Well, never mind; it is almost midnight, and time for all reasonable people to –'

(Louise, rising and throwing her arms around me.) 'Well, I don't choose to be reasonable, and I mean to eclipse the memory of those penny chestnuts and all that sugar and water!' (Pushing me hastily into my study, and locking the door.)

'What the deuce is the matter with you, my dear?' I cried from the other side of the partition.

'Give me ten minutes, no more. Your book is on the mantelpiece; you have not seen it tonight. You will find the matches in the corner.'

Then I heard the rattle of china, the rustle of silky stuffs. Could my wife have gone crazy? At the end of about ten minutes she unlocked the door.

'Don't scold me for shutting you out,' said she, embracing me. 'Look at me. Have I not made myself beautiful? See! My hair just as you like it, high, and my neck uncovered. But my poor neck is so extremely shy that it never could have displayed itself in the broad light, if I had not encouraged it a little by wearing a low-necked gown. After all, it is only right to be in full dress uniform at a supper with the authority.'

'What supper?'

'Why, our supper. My supper with you, of course. Don't you see my illumination and the table covered with flowers and good things to eat? I had it all ready in the alcove; but, you see, to push the table before the fire and make something of a toilet, I had to be alone. I have a big drop of old Chambertin for you. Come, Monsieur, come to supper; I am as hungry as a bear! May I offer you this chicken wing?'

'This is a charming idea of yours, my love, but I really feel ashamed of myself, in my dressing gown.'

'Take it off, sir, if you are uncomfortable, but do not leave me with this chicken wing on my hands. Wait a minute, I want to wait upon you myself.' And rising, she swung her napkin over her arm and pulled up her sleeve to her elbow. 'Isn't that the way the waiters do at the restaurants, tell me?'

'Exactly. But stop a moment, waiter; will you permit me to kiss your hand?'

'I haven't time,' she said, smiling, and she drove the

corkscrew bravely into the neck of a bottle. 'Chambertin! A pretty name. And, besides, do you remember, before we were married – *sapristi*, what a hard cork! – you told me you liked it on account of a play by Alfred de Musset? Which you never gave me to read, by the way. Do you see those little Bohemian glass tumblers that I bought especially for tonight? We will drink each other's health in them.'

'And his too, eh?'

'The heir's, you mean? Poor little love of an heir, I should think so! Then I shall hide the two glasses and bring them out again this day next year, eh, dear? They will be the Christmas supper glasses, and we will have supper every year before the hearth, you and I alone, until our very old, old age.'

'Yes, but when we shall have lost all our teeth –'

'Never mind, we shall have nice little soups, and it will none the less be very sweet. Another piece for me, please, with a little jelly, thank you.'

As she held out her plate to me, I caught a glimpse of her arm, the pretty contours of which disappeared in the lace.

'What are you looking up my sleeve for instead of eating?'

'I am looking at your arm, dear. You are exquisitely pretty tonight; do you know it? Your hair is wonderfully becoming, and that gown! I had never seen that gown before.'

'*Dame!* When a person starts out to make a conquest!'

'You are adorable!'

'Are you quite sure that I am adorable tonight, charming, ravishing?' Then, looking at her bracelet attentively, 'In that case I don't see why, I don't see –'

'What is it that you don't see, dear?'

'I don't see why you don't come and kiss me.'

And as the kiss was prolonged, she threw her head back, showing the double row of her pretty white teeth, exclaiming between her peals of laughter.

'Give me some more pâté! I want some more pâté! Take care! You are going to break my Bohemian glass, the fruit of my economy! There is always some disaster when you try to kiss me. You remember at Madame de Brill's ball, two nights before we were married, how you tore my gown while we were waltzing in the little parlour?'

'Well, but it is very difficult to do two things at once, keep time with the music and kiss your partner.'

'I remember when Mamma asked me how I tore my gown, I felt that I was blushing up to the roots of my hair. And Madame D., that old yellow witch, said to me with her Lenten smile, "What a brilliant colour you have tonight, my child!" I could have choked her! I said I had caught my gown on a nail in the door. I was watching you out of the corner of my eye. You were twirling your moustache, and you seemed quite vexed. You keep all the truffles for yourself, how nice of you! Not that one; I want that big black one there, in the corner. Well, after all, it was none the less very wrong, because no, no, don't fill my glass; I don't want to get tipsy because if we had not married (that might have happened, you know; they say that marriages hang by a thread), well, if the thread had not been strong enough, here I was left with that kiss on my shoulder, a pretty plight!'

'Nonsense! It does not stain.'

'Yes, sir, it does; I beg your pardon, but it does stain, and so much so that there are husbands, I am told, who spill their blood to wash out those little stains.'

'I was only jesting, dear. Heavens! I should think it did! Fancy! Why –'

'Ah, I am glad to hear you say so. I like to see you get angry. You are just a wee bit jealous, tell me, are you not? Well, upon my word! I asked you for the big black one, and you are quietly eating it!'

'I am very sorry, my love; I beg your pardon. I forgot all about it.'

'Yes, just as you did when we were being married. I was obliged to touch your elbow to make you answer yes to Monsieur the Mayor's kind words!'

'Kind words?'

'Yes, kind words. I thought the mayor was charming. No one could have been more happy than he was in addressing me. "Mademoiselle, do you consent to take this great big

ugly little man who stands beside you for your lawful –
(Laughing with her mouth full.) I was about to say to him,
"Let us understand each other, Monsieur; there is much to
be said for and against." Heavens! I am choking! (Bursts into
great peals of laughter.) I was wrong in not making some
restrictions. There! I am teasing you, and that is stupid. I said
yes with my whole heart, I assure you, my darling, and the
word was only too weak. When I think that all women, even
the bad ones, use that same word, I feel ashamed of not
having invented a better one. (Holding up her glass.) Here is
to our golden wedding!'

'And here is to his christening, little mother!'

In an undertone: 'Tell me, dear, are you sorry you married
me?'

(Laughing.) 'Yes. (Kissing her on the shoulder.) I think I
have found the stain. Here it is.'

'Do you realise that it is two o'clock. The fire is out.
I am – you won't laugh? Well, I am just a little dizzy!'

'That was a famous pâté.'

'A famous pâté! We will have a cup of tea in the morning,
eh, dear?'

1870

THE LOST CHILD

François Coppée

On that morning, which was the morning before Christmas, two important events happened simultaneously – the sun rose, and so did M. Jean-Baptiste Godefroy.

Unquestionably the sun, illuminating suddenly the whole of Paris with its morning rays, is an old friend, regarded with affection by everybody. It is particularly welcome after a fortnight of misty atmosphere and grey skies, when the wind has cleared the air and allowed the sun's rays to reach the earth again. Besides all of which the sun is a person of importance. Formerly, he was regarded as a god, and was called Osiris, Apollyon, and I don't know what else. But do not imagine that because the sun is so important he is of greater influence than M. Jean-Baptiste Godefroy, millionaire banker, director of the Comptoir Général de Crédit, administrator of several big companies, deputy and member of the General Counsel of the Eure, officer of the Legion of Honor, etc., etc. And whatever opinion the sun may have about himself, he certainly has not a higher opinion than M. Jean-Baptiste Godefroy has of himself. So we are authorised to state, and we consider ourselves justified in stating, that on the morning in question, at about a quarter to eight, the sun and M. Jean-Baptiste Godefroy rose.

Certainly the manner of rising of these two great powers mentioned was not the same. The good old sun began by doing a great many pretty actions. As the sleet had, during the night, covered the bare branches of the trees in the Boulevard Malesherbes, where the Godefroy townhouse is situated, with a powdered coating, the great magician sun amused himself by transforming the branches into great bouquets of red coral. At the same time he scattered his rays impartially on those poor passers-by whom necessity sent out, so early in the morning, to gain their daily bread. He even had a smile for the poor clerk, who, in a thin overcoat, was hurrying to his office, as well as for the grisette, shivering under her thin, insufficient clothing; for the workman carrying half a loaf under his arm, for the car-conductor as he punched the tickets, and for the dealer in roast chestnuts, who was roasting his first panful. In short, the sun gave pleasure to everybody in the world. M. Jean-Baptiste Godefroy, on the contrary, rose in quite a different frame of mind. On the previous evening he had dined with the Minister for

Agriculture. The dinner, from the removal of the potage to the salad, bristled with truffles, and the banker's stomach, aged forty-seven years, experienced the burning and biting of pyrosis. So the manner in which M. Jean-Baptiste Godefroy rang for his *valet de chambre* was so expressive, that as he got some warm water for his master's shaving, Charles said to the kitchen-maid:

'There he goes! The monkey is barbarously ill-tempered again this morning. My poor Gertrude, we're going to have a miserable day.'

Whereupon, walking on tiptoe, with eyes modestly cast down, he entered the chamber of his master, opened the curtains, lit the fire, and made all the necessary preparations for the toilette, with the discreet demeanour and respectful gestures of a sacristan placing the sacred vessels on the altar for the priest.

'What sort of weather this morning?' demanded M. Godefroy curtly, as he buttoned his undervest of grey swan down upon a stomach that was already a little too prominent.

'Very cold, sir,' replied Charles meekly. 'At six o'clock the thermometer marked seven degrees above zero. But, as you will see, sir, the sky is quite clear, and I think we are going to have a fine morning.'

In stropping his razor, M. Godefroy approached the window, drew aside one of the hangings, looked on the boulevard, which was bathed in brightness, and made a slight grimace which bore some resemblance to a smile.

It is all very well to be perfectly stiff and correct, and to know that it is bad taste to show feeling of any kind in the presence of domestics, but the appearance of the roguish sun, in the middle of December, sends such a glow of warmth to the heart that it is impossible to disguise the fact. So M. Godefroy deigned, as before observed, to smile. If some-one had whispered to the opulent banker that his smile had anything in common with that of the printer's boy, who was enjoying himself by making a slide on the pavement, M. Godefroy would have been highly incensed. But it really was so, all the same; and during the space of one minute this man, who was so occupied by business matters, this leading light in the financial and political worlds, indulged in the childish pastime of watching the passers-by, and following with his eyes the files of conveyances as they gaily rolled in the sunshine.

But pray do not be alarmed. Such a weakness could not last long. People of no account, and those who have nothing to do, may be able to let their time slip by in doing nothing. It is very well for women, children, poets, and riff-raff. M. Gode-froy had other fish to fry; and the work of the day which was commencing promised to be exceptionally heavy. From half past eight to ten o'clock he had a meeting at his office with a certain number of gentlemen, all of whom bore a striking resemblance to M. Godefroy. Like him, they were very agitated; they had risen with the sun, and like him lacked freshness in their souls, and they all had the same object in view – to gain money. After breakfast (which he took after the meeting), M. Godefroy had to leap into his carriage and rush to the Bourse to exchange a few words with other gentlemen who had also risen at dawn, but who had not the least spark of imagination among them. (The conversations were always on the same subject – money.) From there, without losing an instant, M. Godefroy went to preside over another meeting of acquaintances entirely void of compassion and tenderness. The meeting was held around a baize-covered table, which was strewn with heaps of papers and well provided with inkwells. The conversation again turned on money, and various methods of gaining it. After the aforesaid meeting he, in his capacity of deputy, had to appear before several commissions (always held in rooms where there were baize-covered tables and inkwells and heaps of papers). There he found men as devoid of sentiment as he was, all utterly incapable of neglecting any occasion of gaining money, but who, nevertheless, had the extreme goodness to sacrifice several hours of the afternoon to the glory of France.

After having quickly shaved he donned a morning suit, the elegant cut and finish of which showed that the old beau of nearly fifty had not ceased trying to please. When he shaved he spared the narrow strip of pepper-and-salt beard around his chin, as it gave him the air of a trustworthy family man in the eyes of the Auvergnats and of fools in general. Then he descended to his cabinet, where he received the file of men who were entirely occupied by one thought – that of augmenting their capital. These gentlemen discussed several projected enterprises, all of them of considerable import-ance, notably that of a new railroad to be laid across a wild desert. Another scheme was for the founding of a monstrous factory in the environs of Paris, another of a mine to be worked in one of the South American republics. It goes without saying that no one asked if the railway would have passengers or goods to carry, or if the proposed factory should manufacture cotton nightcaps or distil whiskey; whether the mine was to be of virgin gold or of second-rate copper: certainly not. The conversation of M. Godefroy's morning callers turned exclusively upon the profits which it would be possible to realise during the week which should follow the issue of the shares. They discussed particularly the values of the shares, which they knew would be destined before long to be worth less than the paper on which they were printed in fine style.

These conversations, bristling with figures, lasted till ten o'clock precisely, and then the director of the Comptoir

Général de Crédit, who, by the way, was an honest man – at least, as honest as is to be found in business – courteously conducted his last visitor to the head of the stairway. The visitor named was an old villain, as rich as Croesus, who, by a not uncommon chance, enjoyed the general esteem of the public; whereas, had justice been done to him, he would have been lodging at the expense of the state in one of those large establishments provided by a thoughtful government for smaller delinquents; and there he would have pursued a useful and healthy calling for a lengthy period, the exact length having been fixed by the judges of the supreme court. But M. Godefroy showed him out forcefully, notwithstanding his importance – it was absolutely necessary to be at the Bourse at 11 o'clock – and went into the dining room.

It was a luxuriously furnished room. The furniture and silver would have served to endow a cathedral. Nevertheless, notwithstanding that M. Godefroy took a gulp of bicarbonate of soda, his indigestion refused to subside; consequently the banker could take only the scantiest breakfast – that of a dyspeptic. In the midst of such luxury, and under the eye of a well-paid butler, M. Godefroy could eat only a couple of boiled eggs, and nibble a little mutton-chop. The man of money trifled with dessert – took 'only a crumb of Roquefort – not more than two cents' worth.' Then the door opened and an overdressed but charming little child – young Raoul, four years old – the son of the company director, entered the room, accompanied by his German nursery governess.

This event occurred every day at the same hour – a quarter to eleven, precisely, while the carriage which was to take the banker to the Bourse was awaiting the gentleman who had only a quarter of an hour to give to paternal sentiment. It was not that he did not love his son. He did love him – nay, he adored him, in his own particular way. But then, you know, business is business.

At the age of forty-two, when already worldly-wise and blasé, he had fancied himself in love with the daughter of one of his club friends – Marquis de Neufontaine, an old rascal – a nobleman, but one whose card playing was more than open to suspicion, and who would have been expelled from the club more than once, but for the influence of M. Godefroy. The nobleman was only too happy to become the father-in-law of a man who would pay his debts, and without any scruples he handed over his daughter – a simple and ingenuous child of seventeen, who was taken from a convent to be married – to the worldly banker. The girl was certainly sweet and pretty, but she had no dowry except numerous aristocratic prejudices and romantic illusions, and her father thought he was fortunate in getting rid of her on such favourable terms. M. Godefroy, who was the son of an avowed old miser of Andelys, had always remained a man of

the people, and intensely vulgar. In spite of his improved circumstances, he had not improved. His entire lack of tact and
refinement was painful to his young wife, whose tenderest
feelings he ruthlessly and thoughtlessly trampled upon.
Things were looking unpromising, when, happily for her,
Madame Godefroy died in giving birth to her firstborn.
When he spoke of his deceased wife, the banker waxed poetical, although, had she lived, they would have been divorced
in six months. His son he loved dearly for several reasons –
first, because the child was an only son; secondly, because he
was a scion of two such houses as Godefroy and Neufontaine; finally, because the man of money had naturally great
respect for the heir to many millions. So the youngster had
golden rattles and other similar toys, and was brought up like
a young dauphin. But his father, overwhelmed with business
worries, could never give the child more than fifteen minutes
per day of his precious time – and, as on the day mentioned,
it was always during the cheese course at the end of the
meal – and for the rest of the day the father abandoned the
child to the care of the servants.

'Good morning, Raoul.'

'Good morning, Papa.'

And the company director, having put his serviette away,
sat young Raoul on his left knee, took the child's head
between his big paws, and in stroking and kissing it actually

forgot all his money matters and even his note of the afternoon, which was of great importance to him, as by it he could gain quite an important amount of patronage.

'Papa,' said little Raoul suddenly, 'will Father Christmas put anything in my shoe tonight?'

The father answered with 'Yes, if you are a good child.' This was very striking from a man who was a pronounced freethinker, who always applauded every anticlerical attack in the Chamber with a vigorous 'Hear, hear.' He made a mental note that he must buy some toys for his child that very afternoon.

Then he turned to the nursery governess with:

'Are you quite satisfied with Raoul, Mademoiselle Bertha?'

Mademoiselle Bertha became as red as a peony at being addressed, as if the question were scarcely *comme il faut*, and replied by a little imbecile snigger, which seemed fully to satisfy M. Godefroy's curiosity about his son's conduct.

'It's fine today,' said the financier, 'but cold. If you take Raoul to Parc Monceau, mademoiselle, please be careful to wrap him up well.'

Mademoiselle, by a second fit of idiotic smiling, set at rest M. Godefroy's doubts and fears on that essential point. He kissed his child, left the room hastily, and in the hall was enveloped in his fur coat by Charles, who also closed the carriage door. Then the faithful fellow went off to the café which he frequented, rue de Miromesnil, where he had promised to meet the coachman of the baroness who lived opposite, to play a game of billiards, thirty up – and spot-barred, of course.

Thanks to the brown bay horse – for which a thousand francs over and above its value was paid by M. Godefroy as a result of a sumptuous snail supper given to that gentleman's coachman by the horse dealer – thanks to the expensive brown bay which certainly moved along well, the financier was able to get through his many engagements satisfactorily. He appeared punctually at the Bourse, sat at several committee tables, and at a quarter to five, by voting with the ministry, he helped to reassure France and Europe that the rumours of a ministerial crisis had been totally unfounded. He voted with the ministry because he had succeeded in obtaining the favours which he demanded as the price of his vote.

After he had thus nobly fulfilled his duty to himself and his country, M. Godefroy remembered what he had said to his child on the subject of Father Christmas, and gave his coachman the address of a dealer in toys. There he bought, and had put in his carriage, a fantastic rocking horse, mounted on castors – a whip in each ear; a box of leaden soldiers – all as exactly alike as those grenadiers of the Russian regiment of the time of Paul I, who all had black hair and snub noses; and a score of other toys, all equally striking and costly.

Then, as he returned home, softly reposing in his well-swung carriage, the rich banker, who, after all, was a father, began to think with pride of his little boy and to form plans for his future.

When the child grew up he should have an education worthy of a prince, and he would be one, too, for there was no longer any aristocracy except that of money, and his boy would have a capital of about 30,000,000 francs. If his father, a pettifogging provincial lawyer, who had formerly dined in the Latin Quarter when in Paris, who had remarked every evening when putting on a white tie that he looked as fine as if he were going to a wedding – if he had been able to accumulate an enormous fortune, and to become thereby a power in the republic, if he had been able to obtain in marriage a young lady, one of whose ancestors had fallen at Marignan, what an important personage little Raoul might have become. M. Godefroy imagined an array of grand futures for his boy, forgetting that Christmas is the birthday of a very poor little child, son of a couple of vagrants, born in a stable, where the parents found lodging only through charity.

In the midst of the banker's dreams the coachman cried, 'Door, please,' and drove into the yard. As he went up the steps M. Godefroy was thinking that he had barely time to dress for dinner; but on entering the vestibule he found all the domestics crowded in front of him in a state of alarm and confusion. In a corner, crouching on a seat, was the German nursery governess, crying. When she saw the banker she buried her face in her hands and wept still more copiously than before. M. Godefroy felt that some misfortune had happened.

'What's the meaning of all this? What's amiss? What has happened?'

Charles, the valet de chambre, a sneaking rascal of the worst type, looked at his master with eyes full of pity and stammered:

'Monsieur Raoul —'

'My boy?'

'Lost, sir. The stupid German did it. Since four o'clock this afternoon he has not been seen.'

The father staggered back like one who had been hit by a ball. The German threw herself at his feet screaming, 'Mercy, mercy!' and the domestics all spoke at the same time.

'Bertha didn't go to Parc Monceau. She lost the child over there on the fortifications. We have sought him all over, sir. We went to the office for you, sir, and then to the Chamber, but you had just left. Just imagine, the German had a rendezvous with her lover every day, beyond the ramparts, near the gate of Asnières. What a shame! It is a place full of low gypsies and strolling players. Perhaps the child has been stolen. Yes, sir, we informed the police at once. How could we imagine such a thing? A hypocrite, that German! She had a rendezvous, doubtless, with a countryman – a Prussian spy, sure enough!'

His son lost! M. Godefroy seemed to have a torrent of blood rushing through his head. He sprang at Mademoiselle, seized her by the arms and shook her furiously.

'Where did you lose him, you miserable girl? Tell me the truth before I shake you to pieces. Do you hear? Do you hear?'

But the unfortunate girl could only cry and beg for mercy.

The banker tried to be calm. No, it was impossible. Nobody would dare to steal his boy. Somebody would find him and bring him back. Of that there could be no doubt. He could scatter money about right and left, and could have the entire police force at his orders. And he would set to work at once, for not an instant should be lost.

'Charles, don't let the horses be taken out. You others, see that this girl doesn't escape. I'm going to the Prefecture.'

And M. Godefroy, with his heart thumping against his sides as if it would break them, his hair wild with fright, darted into his carriage, which at once rolled off as fast as the horses could take it. What irony! The carriage was full of glittering playthings, which sparkled every time a gaslight shone on them. For the next day was the birthday of the divine Infant at whose cradle wise men and simple shepherds alike adored.

'My poor little Raoul. Poor darling! Where is my boy?' repeated the father as in his anguish he dug his nails into the cushions of the carriage. At that moment all his titles and decorations, his honours, his millions, were valueless to him. He had one single idea burning in his brain. 'My poor child! Where is my child?'

At last he reached the Prefecture of Police. But no one was there – the office had been deserted for some time.

'I am M. Godefroy, deputy from the Eure region . . . My little boy is lost in Paris; a child of four years. I must see the Prefect.'

He slipped a louis into the hand of the concierge.

The good old soul, a veteran with a grey mustache, less for the sake of the money than out of compassion for the poor father, led him to the Prefect's private apartments. M. Godefroy was finally ushered into the room of the man in whom were centred all his hopes. He was in evening dress, and wore a monocle; his manner was frigid and rather pretentious. The distressed father, whose knees trembled through emotion, sank into an armchair, and, bursting into tears, told of the loss of his boy – told the story stammeringly and with many breaks, for his voice was choked by sobs.

The prefect, who was also father of a family, was inwardly moved at the sight of his visitor's grief, but he repressed his emotion and assumed a cold and self-important air.

'You say, sir, that your child has been missing since four o'clock.'

'Yes.'

'Just when night was falling, confound it. He isn't at all precocious, speaks very little, doesn't know where he lives, and can't even pronounce his own name?'

'Unfortunately that is so.'

'Not far from Asnières gate? A dubious quarter. But cheer up. We have a very intelligent *Commissaire de Police* there. I'll telephone to him.'

The distressed father was left alone for five minutes. How his temples throbbed and his heart beat! Then, suddenly, the prefect reappeared, smiling with satisfaction.

'Found!'

Whereupon M. Godefroy rushed to the prefect, whose hand he pressed till that functionary winced with the pain.

'I must acknowledge that we were exceedingly fortunate. The little boy is blond, isn't he? Rather pale? In blue velvet? Black felt hat, with a white feather in it?'

'Yes, yes; that's he. That's my little Raoul.'

'Well, he's at the house of a poor fellow down in that quarter who had just been at the police office to make his declaration to the Commissaire. Here's his address, which I took down: "Pierron, rue des Cailloux, Levallois-Perret." With good horses you may reach your boy in less than an hour. Certainly, you won't find him in an aristocratic quarter; his surroundings won't be of the highest. The man who found him is only a small dealer in vegetables.'

But that was of no importance to M. Godefroy, who, having expressed his gratitude to the prefect, leaped down the stairs four at a time, and sprang into his carriage. At that moment he realised how devotedly he loved his child. As he drove away he no longer thought of little Raoul's princely education and magnificent inheritance. He was decided never again to hand over the child entirely to the hands of servants, and he also made up his mind to devote less time to monetary matters and the glory of France and attend more to his own. The thought also occurred to him that France wouldn't be likely to suffer from the neglect. He had hitherto been ashamed to recognise the existence of an old maid sister of his father, but he decided to send for her to his house. She would certainly shock his lackeys by her primitive manners and ideas. But what of that? She would take care of his boy, which to him was of much more importance than the good opinion of his servants. The financier, who was always in a hurry, never felt so eager to arrive punctually at a committee meeting as he was to reach the lost little one. For the first time in his life he was longing through pure affection to take the child in his arms.

The carriage rolled rapidly along in the clear, crisp night

air down Boulevard Malesherbes; and, having crossed the ramparts and passed the large houses, plunged into the quiet solitude of suburban streets. When the carriage stopped M. Godefroy saw a wretched hovel, on which was the number he was seeking; it was the house where Pierron lived. The door of the house opened immediately, and a big, rough-looking fellow with a red moustache appeared. One of his sleeves was empty. Seeing the gentleman in the carriage, Pierron said cheerily: 'So you are the little one's father. Don't be afraid. The little darling is quite safe,' and, stepping aside in order to allow M. Godefroy to pass, he placed his finger on his lips with: 'Hush! The little one is asleep!'

Yes, it was a real hovel. By the dim light of a little oil lamp M. Godefroy could just distinguish a dresser from which a drawer was missing, some broken chairs, a round table on which stood a beer mug which was half empty, three glasses, some cold meat on a plate, and on the bare plaster of the wall two gaudy pictures – a bird's-eye view of the Exposition of 1889, with the Eiffel Tower in bright blue, and the portrait of General Boulanger as a handsome young lieutenant. This last evidence of weakness of the tenant of the house may well be excused, since it was shared by nearly everybody in France. The man took the lamp and went on tiptoe to the corner of the room where, on a clean bed, two little fellows were fast asleep. In the little one, around whom the other had thrown a protecting arm, M. Godefroy recognised his son.

'The youngsters were tired to death, and so sleepy,' said Pierron, trying to soften his rough voice. 'I had no idea when you would come, so I gave them some supper and put them to bed, and then I went to make a declaration at the police office. Zidore generally sleeps up in the garret, but I thought they would be better here, and that I should be better able to watch them.'

M. Godefroy, however, scarcely heard the explanation. Strangely moved, he looked at the two sleeping infants on an iron bedstead and covered with an old blanket which had once been used either in barracks or hospital. Little Raoul, who was still in his velvet suit, looked so frail and delicate compared with his companion, that the banker almost envied the latter his brown complexion.

'Is he your boy?' he asked Pierron.

'No,' answered he. 'I am a bachelor, and don't suppose I shall ever marry, because of my accident. You see, a dray passed over my arm – that was all. Two years ago a neighbour of mine died, when that child was only five years old. The poor mother really died of starvation. She wove wreaths for the cemeteries, but could make nothing worth mentioning at that trade – not enough to live. However, she worked for the child for five years, and then the neighbours had to buy wreaths for her. So I took care of the youngster. Oh, it was nothing much, and I was soon repaid. He is seven years old, and is a sharp little fellow, so he helps me a great deal. On Sundays and Thursdays, and the other days after school, he helps me push my handcart. Zidore is a smart little chap. It was he who found your boy.'

'What!' exclaimed M. Godefroy, 'that child!'

'Oh, he's quite a little man, I assure you. When he left school he found your child, who was walking on ahead, crying like a fountain. He spoke to him and comforted him, like an old grandfather. The difficulty is, that one can't easily understand what your little one says: English words are mixed up with German and French. So we couldn't get much out of him, nor could we learn his address. Zidore brought him to me – I wasn't far away; and then all the old women in the place came around chattering and croaking like so many frogs, and all full of advice.

'"Take him to the police,"' said some.

'But Zidore protested. "That would scare him," said he, for, like all Parisians, he has no particular liking for the police – "and besides, your little one didn't wish to leave him. So I came back here with the children as soon as I could. They had supper, and then off to bed. Don't they look sweet?" When he was in his carriage, M. Godefroy had decided to reward the finder of his child handsomely – to give him a handful of that gold so easily gained. Since entering the house he had seen a side of human nature with which he was formerly unacquainted – the brave charity of the poor in their misery. The courage of the poor girl who had worked herself to death weaving wreaths to keep her child, the generosity of the poor cripple in adopting the orphan, and above all, the intelligent goodness of the little street urchin in protecting the child who was still smaller than himself – all this touched M. Godefroy deeply and set him reflecting. For the thought had occurred to him that there were other cripples who needed to be looked after as well as Pierron, and other orphans as well as Zidore. He also debated whether it would not be better to employ his time looking after them, and whether money might not be put to a better use than merely gaining more money. Such was his reverie as he stood looking at the two sleeping children. Finally, he turned around to study the features of the greengrocer, and was charmed by the loyal expression in the face of the man, and his clear, truthful eyes.

'My friend,' said M. Godefroy, 'you and your adopted son have rendered me an immense service. I shall soon prove to you that I am not ungrateful. But, for today – I see that you are not in comfortable circumstances, and I should like to leave a small proof of my thankfulness.'

But the lone hand of the cripple stopped the arm of the

banker, who was plunging into his coat pocket where he kept banknotes.

'No, sir; no! Anybody else would have done just as we have done. I will not accept any recompense; but pray don't take offence. Certainly, I am not rolling in wealth, but please excuse my pride – that of an old soldier; I have the Tonquin medal in a drawer – and I don't wish to eat food which I haven't earned.'

'As you like,' said the financier; 'but an old soldier like you is capable of something better. You are too good to push a handcart. I will make some arrangement for you, never fear.'

The cripple responded by a quiet smile, and said coldly: 'Well, sir, if you really wish to do something for me –'

'You'll let me care for Zidore, won't you?' cried M. Godefroy, eagerly.

'That I will, with the greatest of pleasure,' responded Pierron, joyfully. 'I have often thought about the child's future. He is a sharp little fellow. His teachers are delighted with him.'

Then Pierron suddenly stopped, and an expression came over his face which M. Godefroy at once interpreted as one of distrust. The thought evidently was: 'Oh, when he has once left us he'll forget us entirely.'

'You can safely pick the child up in your arms and take him to the carriage. He'll be better at home than here, of course. Oh, you needn't be afraid of disturbing him. He is fast asleep, and you can just pick him up. He must have his shoes on first, though.'

Following Pierron's glance M. Godefroy perceived on the hearth, where a scanty coke fire was dying out, two pairs of children's shoes – the elegant ones of Raoul, and the rough ones of Zidore. Each pair contained a little toy and a package of bonbons.

'Don't think about that,' said Pierron in an abashed tone. 'Zidore put the shoes there. You know children still believe in Christmas and the child Jesus, whatever scholars may say about fables; so, as I came back from the commissaire, as I didn't know whether your boy would have to stay here tonight, I got those things for them both.'

At which the eyes of M. Godefroy, the freethinker, the hardened capitalist, and blasé man of the world, filled with tears.

He rushed out of the house, but returned in a minute with his arms full of the superb mechanical horse, the box of leaden soldiers, and the rest of the costly playthings bought by him in the afternoon, and which had not even been taken out of the carriage.

'My friend, my dear friend,' said he to the greengrocer, 'see, these are the presents which Christmas has brought to my little Raoul. I want him to find them here, when he awakens, and to share them with Zidore, who will henceforth be his playmate and friend. You'll trust me now, won't you? I'll take care both of Zidore and of you, and then I shall ever remain in your debt, for not only have you found my boy, but you have also reminded me, who am rich and lived only for myself, that there are other poor who need to be looked after. I swear by these two sleeping children, I won't forget them any longer.'

Such is the miracle which happened on the 24th of December of last year, ladies and gentlemen, in Paris, in the full flow of modern egotism. It doesn't sound likely – that I own; and I am compelled to attribute this miraculous event to the influence of the Divine child who came down to earth nearly nineteen centuries ago to command men to love one another.

1892

THE JUGGLER OF NOTRE DAME

Anatole France

I

In the days of King Louis there was in France a poor juggler of the name of Barnabé, a native of Compiègne, who used to go from city to city playing all sorts of tricks.

Wherever there was a fair he was sure to be seen with his old worn-out carpet spread on the ground, where, after having drawn together a throng of children and loungers by old jokes, which he repeated exactly as he had learned them, he would throw himself into all sorts of strange attitudes and even balance a pewter plate on his nose. The crowd would at first look on carelessly, but when, standing on his hands, he would toss into the air and catch on his feet six copper balls, sparkling in the sun, or, when throwing himself back till his neck touched his heels, he made himself into a living wheel and played with twelve knives, a murmur of admiration would rise from the spectators, and pieces of money would rain down on the carpet.

Notwithstanding, like most people who live by their talents, Barnabé found it very difficult to live. Earning his bread by the sweat of his brow, he bore more than his just proportion of the wretchedness caused by the sin of Adam, our common father, and he could not even work as much as he would have wished, for, in order to show his skill, he needed warm sun and daylight as much as the trees need them to give us fruit and flowers. In the winters he was like a leafless and half-dead tree: the frozen earth was hard to the poor juggler and, like Marie de France's grasshopper, in bad weather he always suffered from cold and hunger. But as he had a pure heart he bore these evils in patience.

He had never reflected on the origins of riches and the inequality of human conditions. He never doubted that as this world is bad, the other must be good. This faith kept up his courage, and he did not follow the example of thievish mountebanks and miscreants who have sold their souls to the devil. He never blasphemed the name of God; he lived uprightly and, though he had no wife of his own, never coveted the wife of his neighbour, considering that woman is the enemy of strong men as appeareth in the story of Samson, told in the Holy Scripture. He was not a drunkard, though he loved a drink when it was warm, but an honest fellow, fearing God and especially devoted to the Holy Virgin, and always when he went into a church he would kneel before her image and say devoutly, 'Madame, take care of my life till it is God's will that I die, and when I am dead, arrange it so that I shall have the joys of Paradise.'

II

Now, one evening of a very rainy day, as he was going along, sad and bent, carrying the copper globes and knives wrapped up in his old carpet and looking for a barn where he might go supperless to sleep, he overtook on the road a monk and greeted him respectfully, and as they kept on they began to talk.

'Comrade,' said the monk, 'how is it that you are dressed in all green? Is it because you are going to play the part of a fool in some mystery?'

'Oh, no, Father,' answered Barnabé, 'such as you see me I am called Barnabé, and I am a juggler by trade. It would be the best trade in the world if only one had something to eat every day.'

'Friend Barnabé,' went on the monk, 'take care what you say. The most beautiful thing in the world is to be a monk, for he celebrates the praises of God, the Virgin, and the saints, and religious life is a perpetual song to the Lord.'

Barnabé answered: 'Father, I confess that I have spoken like an ignorant man. My trade cannot be compared to yours, and although there is merit in dancing with a little coin balanced on a stick at the end of your nose, that merit is much less than yours. I should like to do as you do, Father, and sing the office every day, especially the office of the most Holy Virgin to whom I have vowed a particular devotion. I would willingly give up the art in which I am known from Soissons to Beauvais, in more than six hundred cities and villages, if I could be a monk.'

The juggler's simplicity touched the monk, and as he was not wanting in shrewdness, he recognised in Barnabé one of those men of good will of whom the Lord has said, 'Peace be to them on the earth,' and so he responded, 'Friend Barnabé, come with me, and I will have you accepted in the convent of which I am Prior. He who led Mary to Egypt has led me to you so that I might guide your feet into the way of salvation.'

And thus Barnabé became a monk. In his convent the brothers devoted themselves more than in any other to the worship of the Holy Virgin, each using for her glory all the knowledge and skill which had been given him by God. The Prior as his part wrote books which treated according to scholastic rules the virtues of the Mother of God, and Brother Maurice copied with a masterly hand on parchment these treatises, which Brother Alexander illuminated with fine miniatures. There was the Queen of Heaven on Solomon's throne, at the feet of which watched four lions, while around her glorified head fluttered seven doves typifying the seven gifts of the Spirit – Fear, Godliness, Knowledge, Strength, Counsel, Understanding, and Wisdom. For her companions she had six virgins with golden hair – Humility, Prudence, Modesty, Respect, Virginity, and Obedience. At her feet two little figures, naked and beautifully white, were standing in an attitude of supplication. These represented souls who were imploring, and certainly not in vain, her all-powerful inter-cession for their salvation. Brother Alexander would then paint on another page Eve and Mary together, showing at the same time sin and redemption, the woman humiliated and the virgin exalted. In this book were also to be seen the Well of Living Water, the Fountain, the Lily, the Moon, the Sun, and the enclosed Garden of Solomon's Song, the Gate of Heaven, the City of God, and many pictures of the Virgin.

Brother Marbode was seemingly one of the most loving children of Mary. He spent all his time cutting stone images, so that his beard, eyebrows, and hair were always white with dust, and his eyes perpetually swollen and running with tears, but he was full of strength and joy in spite of his great age, and it was plain to see that the Queen of Paradise was graciously guarding the last days of her child. Marbode sculptured her sitting on a throne, with a nimbus, and he was always careful that the folds of her robe should cover the feet of her of whom the prophet said, 'A garden enclosed is my sister, my spouse.' And then sometimes he would represent her as a graceful child, and she seemed to be saying, 'O Lord, Thou are my Lord.' *Dixi de ventre matris meae: Deus meus es tu.* (Psalm XXI, 11).

In the convent there were also poets, and they would compose in Latin prose and verse hymns in honour of the Blessed Virgin Mary, and there was even one monk from Picardy who used to put the miracle of Our Lady into the language of the common people and in rhyme.

III

When he saw such a rivalry of praises and so great a harvest of tributes, Barnabé was always lamenting his ignorance and stupidity. 'Alas!' he would sigh as he walked alone in the little shadeless garden of the convent, 'I am very unhappy that I cannot, like my brothers, worthily praise the holy Mother of God to whom I have vowed the tenderness of my heart. Alas! Alas! I am a rough man and without skill, and I have for your service, Madame Virgin, neither learned sermons nor treatises divided according to rules, nor fine paintings nor beautifully cut statues, nor verses counted out into feet and marching by measure. I would have nothing, alas!' And then he would groan and give himself up to sadness. One day while the brothers were talking during their recreation he heard one of them tell of a monk who could do nothing but recite the *Ave Maria*. This monk was despised for his ignorance, but when he died there came out of his mouth five roses in honour of the five letters of the name of Maria, and his holiness was thus manifested. As he heard this story, Barnabé once more wondered at the Virgin's goodness, but he was not consoled by the example of the blessed dead monk, for his heart was full of zeal and he longed to exalt the glory of his Lady who is in the heavens.

But he sought in vain for a means of doing this, and he grew day by day more grieved till one morning he awoke full of joy, and running to the chapel, remained there for more than an hour, going back again after dinner. From that time he would go every day to this chapel at an hour when it was empty and he spent there a great part of the time that the other monks consecrated to artistic and ordinary labours. He was no more sad and he no longer groaned.

So singular a change excited the curiosity of the monks, and they began to gossip as to the frequent retreats of Brother Barnabé. The Prior, whose duty it is to pass over nothing in the conduct of his monks without scrutiny, resolved to observe Barnabé in his solitary devotions, and one day when the brother was shut up as usual in the chapel came my Lord

Prior, with two of the oldest brethren, to spy out through the cracks of the door what was going on inside.

Then they saw Barnabé before the altar of the Virgin on his head, his feet in the air, and tossing up and catching again six copper balls and twelve knives. He was playing, in the honour of the holy Mother of God, the tricks which had formerly won him so much praise, but not understanding that this simple man was thus offering up his one talent and his only knowledge to the service of the Holy Virgin, the two old monks cried out at the sacrilege. The Prior knew that Barnabé was incapable of any such thing, but he judged that the poor man had fallen from melancholy into insanity, and they were all three about to drag him by force from the chapel, when they saw the Holy Virgin come down the steps of the altar and gently wipe off with the fold of her beautiful blue robe the drops of sweat which stood thick on the forehead of the juggler.

Then the Prior knelt down with his face on the marble pavement and recited these words: 'Blessed are the simplehearted, for they shall see God.'

'Amen!' answered the reverend monks, kissing the floor.

1892

NOËL

Irène Némirovsky

As the title of the film and list of actors scroll down the screen, we first see appear, initially as a background, then as detailed photographs, all the most conventional and unsophisticated images that accompany the idea of the Christmas holidays.

First, heavy, blinding snow that falls slowly from above. Then it turns to rain, forming a light wintery mist over the streets of Paris.

Garlands of holly and mistletoe turn to dead leaves and are carried away by the flowing water.

A large log disintegrating into sparks cuts to the image of radiators.

A panorama of snow, an idyllic scene, turns into a small street in Montmartre, and the songs of children gradually become nasal, unpleasant.

Everywhere, shop signs are shining brightly. Christmas Eve. Dinner parties, etc. The songs become clearer; we recognise words like:

Childhood
Innocence . . .
Dawn of the world . . .
Dawn of love
The most wonderful days . . .

Accompanied by the shrill music of an organ grinder.

The music stops, the vague images disappear and the movie begins.

In a large, dark drawing room, two men are carrying a Christmas tree, still undecorated; its branches drag along the floor. They wipe the sweat from their brows. A valet enters holding a coin.

'Here's your tip.'

The men frown: 'That's it? Well, really now . . .'

The servant shrugs his shoulders. 'Our boss is a real cheapskate . . .'

The men leave, grumbling. On the white walls in front of the door to the pantry, a hand is writing: *The stairs are high, and the tips are low . . .* while a man whistles contemptuously as he goes down the steps. The servant looks at the tree, indifferently gives it a kick to prop it up and leaves the room.

In the hall, two well-dressed children, followed by a nanny, run out of their room.

'Is that the Christmas tree? Is it pretty?' they ask, excited.

'Very pretty, Mademoiselle Christiane, the Christ Child has just brought it,' says the valet, forcing, with difficulty, his sour face into an affectionate grimace.

'Christiane, Jeannot, come along,' the nanny says, sharply, 'What are you doing?'

We catch a glimpse of the large, bare tree in the dark drawing room. Outside the window, the winter rain is falling, mixed with snow, lit up by a streetlight. Then rumbling from the street. Images of Paris on Christmas Eve. Stacks of pine trees tied together on the quayside. Brightly lit signs on the department stores, the shopfronts of *Potin*, *Potel* and *Chabot* weighed down with turkeys and oysters. Pyramids of bottles of champagne, *Chez Nicolas*. The rush of cars and buses; shops selling candy, florists, feverish salesgirls rushing about.

'Two kilos of candied chestnuts . . . a basket of orchids,' etc.

The hustle and bustle of conversations, a record spinning around. Then the street. Dazed little children dragged along by their exhausted parents, some affectionate and happy, others irritable, weary. A serious-looking father with a goatee, holding a skinny little rascal by the ear says with indignation:

'I buy him a car that costs nearly twenty francs. And now little Sir wants a garage to put it in . . . Greed and ingratitude are two terrible vices, my boy . . . And at your age . . .' His voice trails off amid the noise of the crowd.

Other children leap with curiosity around the wrapped packages their parents have under their arms. We hear their joyful chirping:

'Mama, what is Santa Claus going to bring me? Tell me!'

'Santa Claus isn't real, you know,' one little girl says to another, 'it's like the stork; it's really Papa . . .'

Lovers hold each other tight and kiss as they walk by.

Then we see, always very quickly, very rapidly, department store shelves full of toys, Christmas trees, decorated, sparkling, swaying, going round and round. The noise finally dies down. The salespeople hurry, pulling down the iron shutters over the storefronts. The rumbling of Paris grows fainter, distant, ends in silence. In a children's bedroom in front of a small low table, Christiane and Jeannot are colouring Christmas trees. They are humming: 'Three angels came tonight to bring me such wonderful things . . .,' a tune that has gradually been adapted from Chevalier's words, spoken through a record player in the next room. There, Marie-Laure and Claudine, their two older sisters, aged twenty-two and twenty, are getting dressed to go to a ball. Their dresses and fine lingerie are laid out on the bed, amid the chaos of a young woman's bedroom. Marie-Laure is putting on make-up in front of the mirror. Claudine, still wearing her peignoir, is standing at the window, watching the rain, thinking.

'Claudine!' calls Marie-Laure, 'Claudine! Hey! I'm talking to you! Why are you making that face?'

Claudine shudders. 'What?'

'You've had your head in the clouds for some time now . . . Trouble with your love life? Your Ramon? . . . Really, don't make such a fuss . . . Men – they come, they go . . . No importance whatsoever . . . Are you ever going to get dressed? It's nearly nine o'clock . . .'

We see the children again, half asleep in their chairs. The young women slip on their dress shoes, help each other put on their pearls.

The nanny knocks at a door; we hear shrill voices. Monsieur and Madame are getting dressed, and arguing. He is bald, short and ugly. He is in a bad mood and grumbles:

'You slave away just to make ungrateful people rich . . . that's my fate . . . What a stupid custom to go out to celebrate Christmas Eve, poisoning yourself and eating disgusting things at a restaurant instead of staying peacefully at home!'

Madame: she is wearing make-up, worried about her clothes, old and fat.

'If you'd listened to me, we would have gone to the Midi!'

Monsieur breaks a nail putting on one of his cuff-links and impatiently stamps his foot on the floor.

Madame: 'Oh, no, please, go and let off steam somewhere else . . . It's not my fault that it's Christmas, really!'

Monsieur: 'It's the same with this Christmas tree, and the children's tea party . . . It's going to cost a fortune . . . The children don't need all that to enjoy themselves . . . We're giving them a taste for unbridled luxury!'

Madame (bitterly): 'It's not because I enjoy it, you know, but we have to return invitations to people who have invited us, it's only polite . . . And besides, if you'd rather people know you're about to go bankrupt!'

Monsieur (horrified): 'Shh, shh . . .'

They finally hear the nanny discreetly knocking at the door.

'Who's there? Come in . . .'

The Nanny: 'It's nine o'clock. The children are falling asleep.'

'Well, then put them to bed.'

'But . . . they want to hang their stockings in front of the fireplace . . . They've been waiting since seven o'clock.'

Madame: 'Oh, my God, yes. I'd forgotten, bring them in.'

Christiane and Jeannot enter, in their pajamas, holding their stockings.

The children kiss their parents, put their stockings over the fireplace and kneel down.

'Dear Jesus, please bring me a real donkey, a train set with tracks and a little brother 'cause there's too many girls in this house.'

Meanwhile, his father, who is having a bit of trouble putting on his boots because of his fat stomach, interrupts him:

'All right, all right, that's enough, dear Jesus is not very rich this year, my boy.'

Madame, who had been moved at first, has lost interest. 'Yes, tighter,' she says to her maid who is lacing up her corset, 'tighter, it's fine.'

'But Madame, there's no way.'

'Yes, there is.'

Then, annoyed, looking at herself in the mirror: 'My God, this dress makes me look so fat.'

The frame fades. Far-off music plays: 'Three angels came tonight . . .'

A fireplace full of toys – miniature trumpets and toy dolls – appears in the darkness; they transform into real trumpets and live dolls in a nightclub.

Dancing, jazz, drunkards, dust, etc.

Meanwhile, Marie-Laure and Claudine and their parents are in the car, their father and mother in the back, the two young women wearing bright dresses, ball gowns decorated with ermine, sit in the front. Monsieur and Madame continue to argue.

Monsieur: 'What a way to behave . . . Young women these days don't even deign to invite their parents to the parties they give! . . . Very nice, very appropriate, you have to admit.'

Marie-Laure (annoyed): 'But, Papa, I told you that Nadine's mother and aunt will be there; I should think that's enough!'

Monsieur (without listening to her): 'Really, this habit of letting young women come home by themselves, at God knows at what time, accompanied by such scoundrels!'

Madame: 'Well, then you can go and pick them up yourself!'

Marie-Laure: 'Actually, Édouard Saulnier, from the Saulnier Sugar Factory family is going to bring us home.'

Father (attentive): 'Oh?'

Marie-Laure (mockingly): 'Well, well – that seems to reassure you.'

Father: 'He's obviously a suitable young man.'

Marie-Laure: 'And rich!'

Father: 'You know what I think about that, my dears . . . For a marriage to be truly happy, like your parents' marriage for example, you must be united, understand each other, get along well, be in love, in short . . . like the perfect union we have been giving you as an example since you were children.

Now, considering that business is going from bad to worse, if you both were to marry well . . .'

Madame: 'My God, you really can't wait to get rid of them . . . they're still children . . .'

Father (baulking): 'Are you afraid of becoming a grand-mother, eh, is that it?'

The car stops.

Madame, forcing herself to sound strict as the chauffeur opens the car door: 'I forbid you to come home later than two o'clock. Do you hear me, girls?'

'Yes, Mama.'

In the entrance hall, Marie-Laure pokes her sister: 'Listen, pull yourself together, you look upset.'

Claudine (anxious): 'Really?'

Marie-Laure: 'But what . . . what's wrong?'

Claudine (annoyed): 'Nothing, my God, nothing . . . I was tired but I'm all right now, I'm all right . . .'

Her final words are lost in the general commotion. Laughter, music. A debutante ball. Only very young men and women, everyone very merry. In a little room off to one side, two serene old women – they look like sheep in profile – the lady of the house and her sister, are knitting. Music in the distance. One of the old ladies sighs:

'Ah, how happy the young are . . . It's a pleasure to listen to them! Do you remember, Louise?' (She sighs.)

Claudine goes into the ballroom, anxiously looking for someone among the dancers; she replies to the young people who say hello as they pass by with a smile, a nod. At the same time, a hand slips around her waist. 'Shall we dance?' the voice says. She turns quickly around, recognises Ramon, a handsome, elegant young man.

They dance.

We see the old women again. A laugh that is a little too forced and shrill jazz music have made them start. One of them whispers, worried: 'Perhaps . . . we should go and see . . .'

'The youngsters don't like it when we are obviously watching them, and besides, what can we do? It's us, the adults, with our suspicions who put evil thoughts in their minds.'

The other lady (hesitant): 'All the same, my dear, we're meant to be chaperoning them.'

We see the ballroom where about twenty couples are holding each other tightly and dancing a sensual tango in the semi-darkness.

Nadine, the young lady of the house, wearing very modern clothes, notices her mother and her aunt coming over to them, and tells everyone in a playful whisper: 'Yikes! The cops are here!'

Everyone immediately starts behaving impeccably. The lights are switched on. The jazz band plays a lovely waltz.

The two old women are touched: 'They're so charming.'

The camera pans and reveals little dark corners here and there around the brightly lit ballroom. In one of them, a couple is kissing, in another, all we see is the bottom of a young woman's dress. She is sitting down and her fashionable full skirt is pulled up to her knee, revealing her beautiful legs. As the two old women get closer, the dress is slowly lowered, and we hear a very serene voice, very 'virginal', reply: 'Oh, yes, Madame, thank you so much; we're having such a lovely time . . .'

On the banister of the staircase, two young men are standing very close to a young woman. The old woman comes closer, raises her lorgnette and sweetly asks: 'What game is this you're playing, children? My eyes are so bad, I can't tell.'

'Just an innocent little game, Madame.'

'Oh, really? I didn't know you still played those kinds of games, like I did when I was young . . . Keep going, my dears.'

Meanwhile, Claudine and Ramon are dancing.

'You look especially lovely tonight, Claudine.'

'Oh, Ramon, I've been trying to see you for a week.'

'Oh, I've had a lot on my mind . . . problems,' he says, with a barely noticeable hint of coldness in his voice.

'I needed to speak to you about something important.'

'Oh?' he replies, with a slight gesture of suspicion.

When the two old women appear, they look at Claudine affectionately.

'Look at that little Claudine . . . she's just charming . . . What I especially like about her is how virtuous she looks . . . she looks so 'virginal', don't you think? I was like that when I was young.'

'She and Ramon make a handsome couple. Is she going to marry him?'

'Oh, I don't think so. Nadine told me he already has a fiancée back home, in Buenos Aires. She found out by chance.'

Meanwhile, two young people disappear into a little adjoining room. You can hear music in the distance.

Claudine (secretly): 'I'm going to have a baby, Ramon.'

She is standing, looking very fragile and childlike in her white dress. Ramon makes an irritated gesture and says, faltering: 'Good heavens . . . that's a nuisance.'

Claudine, with a hint of a smile: 'Yes . . . rather.'

In the ballroom, they are giving out streamers and confetti. The dancers form a long chain that stretches from one end of the room to the other and under a door decorated with mistletoe. We see a front view of couples kissing: the good girls who laugh and offer their cheeks, the little sly ones who make sure that the kiss on the cheek ends up near their lips, and, finally, the spinster, going to seed, dressed like a child, who offers her mouth to her doleful cavalier and who, peeved, gets a peck on the forehead. Then Marie-Laure appears with a young man, Édouard Saulnier; he is short, ugly, with a kind, timid appearance. He wants to kiss her.

She pushes him away: 'Oh, no, dear boy!'

Him, annoyed: 'So everyone except me?'

'*You* will have to marry me first . . .'

'Charming . . . And why?'

She sighs. He looks at her with some admiration.

'You have many faults, Marie-Laure, but no one could really accuse you of hiding your feelings.'

She shrugs her shoulders: 'You want to kiss me. *I* don't want you to. It's give-and-take. I'll say it again: marry me. Until then, no kissing.'

Édouard, hissing: 'Little bitch . . .'

'What did you say?'

'Nothing.'

Under the mistletoe, she offers her hand for him to kiss, and little by little, manages to let her arm drift under the young man's nose several times. She laughs, sounding provocative and cunning:

'Still, I think you would prefer Claudine, wouldn't you? Too bad she only has eyes for Ramon, eh? But I'm a nice girl; I know very well that I'm just a consolation prize to you, but I'm not angry about it.'

Claudine and Ramon again. He is holding her hand.

'Listen, my little one . . . we must be reasonable . . . What can you do? It's life . . . that is keeping us apart . . . You know very well that if I could marry you, I would, and with joy . . . with the greatest happiness . . . But my father is uncompromising. I'm leaving . . . (She makes a sudden movement) I'm leaving tomorrow morning, my poor darling, I'm going back home and getting married there . . . I'm so sorry, I swear, so very sorry . . . Oh, we shouldn't have let ourselves get carried away.'

She makes a weary gesture: 'Oh . . .'

'It's true . . . it's true, I blame myself more than you think . . .'

She pulls her hand from his.

'Claudine . . .'

'Leave me alone . . .'

She goes back inside the ballroom. He throws away his cigarette and says with sincere pity: 'Poor girl . . . Good Lord, this is annoying . . . What a problem . . . (he thinks for a moment) If it's true, of course . . .'

Back to the ball. Then to two young women in a corner. One of them tries to stop her stocking from running with a damp finger. 'Damn! A pair of stockings ruined! . . . And Georges still hasn't asked me to marry him . . . What a business it is to be a young woman!'

Ramon, surrounded by a group of young people: 'Well,

my dear friends, I have to say my farewells tonight . . . Yes, I'm leaving tomorrow morning . . .'

'Really?' says a stocky young lad with a grin on his face, 'I thought you weren't leaving until next week.'

Ramon elbows him in the ribs so he stops talking.

We hear: 'Well, goodbye, goodbye, then.'

Now the young women have all come closer and are watching – their eyes bright with curiosity and maliciousness – as Claudine and Ramon are going to say goodbye to each other. Meanwhile, other couples are dancing.

Ramon, embarrassed: 'Goodbye, Claudine . . .'

Claudine looks at him. He lowers his eyes. The young women snigger. She offers him her hand, making a great effort to remain calm.

'Goodbye, Ramon . . . Bon voyage.'

The couples start dancing again, turning round and round. Claudine stands apart, alone. Édouard Saulnier appears behind her.

'What's the matter? You were so cheerful before . . . What's wrong?'

'Nothing, Édouard, it's nothing. Thank you,' she whispers, holding back her tears.

Then pan to the cabaret where her parents have been celebrating. At first, we hear the church bells calling the religious to Midnight Mass, but they are drowned out by the sound of jazz. There are so many people in the nightclub that all we can see are a mass of couples crushed in under a cloud of confetti and streamers that are flying around. We see the points of two paper hats. The hats are taken off, revealing the pitiful face of Claudine's father and another older gentleman.

'Oh, it's horrible, horrible; who would have thought that the Chantace stocks would drop by twenty-five per cent in two months?'

'*I would*, but you didn't listen to me,' says the other man, bitterly.

'But you have some of their stock too!'

'Of course, and that's *your* fault, I was taken in by your blind confidence.'

'We tell ourselves that they can't go any lower . . . which is a mistake . . . We have to get it in our heads that stocks can always go down.'

Streamers landing on his nose make him fall silent. The black musicians twist and turn like contortionists. Meanwhile, Claudine's mother is dancing with an Argentinian, shorter than her, whom she holds tightly, lovingly, in her arms.

'Do you love me?'

Him: A cascade of incomprehensible Castillian *r*'s.

Her (nearly fainting): 'Oh, when you look at me like that, I tremble all over.'

The faithful come out of Midnight Mass. The partygoers leave the restaurant. A drunken man holds his toy dolls close to his heart. When people bump into him, he complains.

'Oh, my little dolls, let me keep my little dolls, you mean people.'

A very small bellboy, as tiny as can be, leads him to his car with maternal care.

'Yes, Monsieur, no one will touch your little dolls, this way, Monsieur . . .'

Once again we see the ballroom where Marie-Laure and her friends are dancing. The young Nadine is cajoling her mother: 'Mama, go up to bed, this is ridiculous, you'll feel awful tomorrow.'

'Well, Nadine, will you all be good?'

Nadine opens her eyes in wide innocence: 'What do you mean, Mama?'

'I mean . . . you won't make too much noise?'

'Oh, no, Mama, I promise.'

Semi-darkness. Songs playing quietly on the record player. Divans, plush armchairs, flirting, kissing.

Nadine: 'Mama made a point of telling us not to make too much noise.'

Laughter.

A young man quietly sings a blues song.

Claudine to Édouard: 'You're a kind friend . . . but it's my fault. I've been stupid. I should have behaved like everyone else here, flirt, rather than fall in love. I didn't know and I only got what I deserve.'

'But . . . Claudine . . .'

Claudine (sharply): 'Oh, don't go imagining anything out of the ordinary happened. No, I admit that I . . . I was very fond of Ramon, and that it hurts that he's leaving . . . so . . .'

Nadine, wearing a top hat, dances, twisting and turning.

Claudine (angrily):

'If I have a daughter, I can tell you she won't be raised like her, or like me!'

Édouard, smiling: 'Well, you have plenty of time to think about that.'

Marie-Laure calls out: 'Édouard, where on earth are you?' Then quietly, angrily, to Claudine: 'Listen, what you're doing is disgusting! We promised each other: I wouldn't go near your Ramon and you wouldn't go near Édouard! Besides, I'm the eldest . . .'

Claudine (quietly): 'Leave me alone, Marie-Laure.'

'You, dear sister, have done something stupid.'

Night-time. We see the brightly lit sign on a department store: Santa Claus is going down a chimney with lots of presents. We can see the windows lit up, the shadows of people dancing. Jeannot and Christiane's room, them in bed. They wake up with a start when the heavy courtyard door noisily opens.

Jeannot: 'Perhaps it's Santa Claus . . .'

Christine: 'You're so stupid, he comes down the chimney, that's the grown-ups coming home.'

Downstairs, Marie-Laure and Claudine come into the entrance hall, on tiptoe.

Marie-Laure: 'Damn! It's after five o'clock. We're going to get told off . . .'

Claudine: 'We have to be quiet.'

Marie-Laure knocks over a piece of furniture, making a terrible noise. They switch on the lights.

'Well, well, our parents aren't home yet,' says Marie-Laure, 'we shouldn't have been so worried.'

We see the servants who are celebrating on the sixth floor.

Then, in the car, their parents, who disappear under a mass of streamers and confetti.

Marie-Laure and Claudine get undressed.

'You know, I think this is it, this time. I told Édouard to come over tomorrow. He asked if Papa would be home.'

Claudine: 'Do you love him?'

Marie-Laure (shrugging her shoulders): 'He's rolling in it . . .'

Claudine (pensively): 'He seems like a good man. You're lucky.'

She starts brushing her hair. Marie-Laure is humming; her sister says, sharply: 'Oh, do be quiet!'

'Mademoiselle is nervous. Oh, of course, that was your Ramon's favourite tango.'

'Yes, it was.'

'Goodness, you really are old-fashioned! We flirt, we part, that's life . . . True love only comes when you're married, and I don't mean with your husband, naturally.'

Claudine drops down onto the bed, sobbing: 'Oh, Marie-Laure, if only you knew! There's nothing more I can do, except kill myself, do you understand?'

Marie-Laure (suddenly very harshly): 'What do you mean?'

'I'm going to have Ramon's baby . . . Ramon . . . who knows and who is going away . . . (a gesture of despair) I loved him, I thought he would marry me, of course, yes, I thought I knew everything, that I was very smart, but I was actually just as stupid as everyone else.'

Marie-Laure (furious): 'What are you going to do?'

'Do you think I know?'

The image fades. We see the parents coming home, in a bad mood.

'What disgusting champagne . . . and who was that little Argentinian who kept dancing with you?'

'A charming young man.'

We see Marie-Laure who is finishing saying something to Claudine; all we can hear is: 'Now listen to me, I'm giving you good advice!' and Claudine who says over and over again: 'No, no, I don't want to . . .'

Fade to the children's bedroom. The first dawn of winter. Christiane, leaning on one elbow, watching, enraptured, the snow that has fallen onto the windowsill during the night. A bird is pecking at something. A perfect Christmas card image. A taxi full of drunkards passes by on the street. In front of the doors to the nightclubs, people are sweeping up piles of streamers, confetti and crushed toy dolls.

Then the first church bells ring. We see families going to Mass. Well-dressed children, wearing white gloves, holding their little prayer books. A light snow is falling. Through the windows of several different houses, we see children in their parents' rooms, on large beds, with new toys. We hear the children shouting and laughing.

Christiane and Jeannot solemnly walk into their parents' bedroom. We see the fireplace full of toys, hear the little ones saying 'oh' in amazement, then, the bed, where their parents—puffed up, snoring, wrinkled – their balding father, and their mother wearing a chin strap, are sleeping. Jeannot is busy playing with his toys, but Christiane looks at her parents, lowers her head and seems upset and unhappy. A sleepy, moaning voice comes from under the covers: 'Take them out, dear Nannie, can't you see I have a headache?'

The servants set the table for the guests who have been

invited to the Christmas party. We see the tall tree decorated with toys.

In her bedroom, their mother, who has recovered somewhat, is now talking to Marie-Laure and Claudine. She gives each of them a little pendant. Claudine, very upset, murmurs as she kisses her: 'Mama . . .'

'Yes?'

'I need to talk to you.'

The mother (annoyed): 'Well, talk fast . . .'

'It's just that . . . it's too difficult . . . this way . . . Mama . . .'

'Well then, we'll do it another time, my child. You can see I'm in a hurry.'

Marie-Laure sniggers as she leaves the room, prodding her sister with her elbow.

'You see? You're still fooling yourself, come on . . . Can you picture Mama raising your kid, and Papa telling you: "Miserable girl; you've disgraced me, but I forgive you!" Well, can you? All *I'm* asking you, and I think I do have a say in all this, is that there be no scandal!'

'What has it got to do with you?'

'Well, that's a good one. What about my marriage?'

The scene fades. Paris, Christmas morning. The shops are closed. In the street, the last pine trees have been taken away; people are sweeping up the needles left on the sidewalk. Trash in Les Halles food market. Then we see how Claudine's parents spend this family holiday. Her father is with his mistress. An insignificant little actress who greets him rather coldly. He says (sounding pitiful): 'I brought you your little Christmas present, my sweetie . . .'

He gives her a pendant exactly like the one given to his daughters. She grumbles: 'Yeah, I see you didn't knock yourself out.'

She's stretched out on the bed in her pajamas. She hangs the pendant from her toe, swings it there for a moment, then kicks it onto the rug. He goes over to her, whispers: 'My Louloute . . .'

She sighs and lets him kiss her.

A barrel organ grinds away in the courtyard:

> *Childhood, innocence*
> *Dawn of life . . .*

Then Christiane and Jeannot appear on a path in the Bois de Boulogne. The voice of the invisible nanny nags them, scolding: 'Christiane, stand up straight . . . Jeannot, don't get your gloves dirty, stop jumping,' etc.

The song continues:

> *Love is for the young*
> *In the springtime, the birds all agree . . .*

Fade to the bachelor pad of the little Argentinian. In the bathroom, Madame is pulling in her bosom with a tight, invisible band made of pink rubber.

Then the voice of the little Argentinian: 'I have so many difficulties . . . My father who owns an enormous farm wrote to me saying that this year, he can't send me my allowance because the bulls won't mate with the cows . . .'

(Superimposed: bulls turn away in disgust when the cows, mooing sadly, pass by.)

The music plays again. Madame sighs: 'Oh, it's so romantic.'

Finally, in a poor neighbourhood, one of those terrible areas where every window has a sign that says DENTIST'S OFFICE in gold letters, we see Claudine walking quickly; she looks weary and desperate. The morning snow has turned into water and mud. A woman offers her a branch of mistletoe.

'It brings happiness, Mademoiselle!'

After Claudine has given her some money and walked away, the woman watches her go and sighs: 'Some people are lucky,' then begins shouting in the gathering fog: 'Mistletoe for happiness! Come and get it! Plenty for everyone!'

Her voice merges with the animated sound of the children gathered around the Christmas tree as it is being lit up. They are playing, singing, dancing. We hear only their voices, their laughter as the doors open very slowly, a fairy tale, mysterious atmosphere, to reveal the magnificent pine tree with hundreds of little lit candles.

In the little adjoining room sit Édouard and Marie-Laure.

Édouard: 'Where is Claudine?'

'She went out.'

'She seemed so sad yesterday.'

'She's been depressed since her Ramon left. It serves her right; she shouldn't have thrown herself at him.'

Claudine is wandering in the street, anxiously looking for an address. Finally, she goes through a door, whispers a name to the concierge who replies with a snigger and a shrug of her shoulders.

'Fifth floor, door on the left.'

Claudine climbs the stairs; we see the look of despair on her face. The staircase is horrible, narrow, dark, with a very small gaslight on the landing, lighting up a shiny sign: MIDWIFE.

Claudine has stopped on the landing. We see only her shadow. At that moment, a young woman comes down holding a baby in her arms. He's a tiny little thing, ugly; he's asleep. As the mother passes by Claudine, she covers, with infinite care, the infant's face with a little gauze veil. Claudine looks at the child, then at the mother, who is an ordinary working-class woman dressed all in black; she then looks at the door. We see her shadow slowly go back down the stairs, and below, on the bright street, she joins a crowd of people rushing about; they all disappear.

Meanwhile, the table is being set for the party.

One of the maids (disgusted): 'Those kids are making such a racket! I have a headache, what a celebration we had last night, didn't we!'

Angelic faces singing an old Christmas song around the piano. Two little boys in sailor suits, their mouths full of cake, are talking: 'They're still boring us to death with their music! Say, do you have the *Auto* magazine? Who won the Schneider Cup?'

In the small living room, Édouard and Marie-Laure are having an argument.

'You gullible fool, really, leave it to you to defend my holier-than-thou sister!'

'Why are you saying that?'

'Because . . .' and she whispers something in his ear.

At that moment, Claudine comes home. The children run across the room and hug her.

'Claudine! It's Claudine! Come and play with us.'

She gently pushes them away, goes into her room and locks the door; they start to follow her, but the Christmas pudding has been lit and appears. We see all their little expressions over their cups of hot chocolate, the nanny scolding them. Claudine is in her room, crushed against the window. She murmurs in a toneless, despairing voice:

'What am I going to do? What am I going to do?'

At that moment, we see her father adjusting his tie in front of the mirror, at his mistress's place. 'So you're sure you won't be able to come back tonight?' she asks, sounding hopeful.

'No, impossible.'

'Oh, good,' she sighs, relieved.

In the entrance hall to the bachelor pad where Claudine's mother meets her lover, we see a hand slipping a small wallet into a man's hand that quickly closes over it.

The image fades into a different hand, Claudine's; she is opening a small flask with the label: barbital.

The children dance around the tree.

Claudine carefully closes the doors and turns on the gas of the hot water tank above the bathtub, in the adjoining bathroom. Then she locks her door again. She walks over to the window, looks outside in despair as if she were hoping for something to come to help her, in vain.

'My God,' she whispers, 'Forgive me; I'm an unfortunate wretch . . .'

She takes the barbital. (All we see is a full glass of water, then empty and the trembling hand holding it.) She lays down on her bed.

IRÈNE NÉMIROVSKY

The children's voices are heard singing in the living room; they soon fade away under the sound of church bells, then return stronger, shrill. (This should give the impression of a nightmare Claudine is having while asleep.) When the singing stops, we clearly hear the sound of gas, like a hissing snake.

Édouard walks over to the children, who are now looking for some hidden object, accompanied by music, childish, obsessive music that is annoying.

He asks Christiane and Jeannot: 'Has your sister come back yet?'

The children barely reply. They are running around in all directions, shouting and talking all at once. The toys are given out; they pull them quite roughly from the branches of the tree and we see the tree shaking. A padded toy Santa Claus, badly attached, falls to the ground and all the little white shoes trample him, indifferent. The governesses blow out the candles. Jeannot, tears in his eyes, protests: 'Oh, what a shame, it was so beautiful!'

The nanny (dryly): 'You're nothing more than a little self-centred child. That's what Christmas trees are for.'

The children, shouting with joy, throw streamers, put on paper hats and blow into the cardboard trumpets. 'A farandole! A farandole!' One of the governesses sits down at the piano and plays vigorously. The children spin around quickly, more and more quickly; they get wild from their game. They run around the tree, then through the whole apartment, rushing through empty rooms and ending up in front of Claudine's door. It is locked and they begin banging on it: 'Let us in, let us in!'

Édouard, who has followed them, asks in surprise: 'What are you doing here?'

'Monsieur, Christiane and Jeannot's sister won't open the door. You see, it's locked.'

'Well, that's because she wants to be left alone.'

'Oh, no, of course not, she's playing a trick on us . . . Otherwise, she would have told us off by now,' replies a chubby-cheeked little boy wearing an Eton uniform.

Suddenly, Édouard is filled with anxiety and asks: 'Have you been calling her for a long time without her answering?'

'Oh, yes, a very long time!'

Édouard starts calling her, quietly at first, then much louder: 'Claudine! Claudine!'

No reply. The children, who have gradually become more and more worried, fall silent. Édouard kicks the door, bangs on it with his fists, but it remains firmly closed.

The hissing of gas. Claudine's head thrown back, her face white. The governess, in the empty living room, is being kissed by the butler but continues playing the piano, oblivious.

Édouard, determined, shouts: 'Be quiet, all of you! G . . . Damn it!'

While he is rattling the door, two of the kids have found a ladder and climbed up to the little skylight cut out of the roof, above the chimney, in Claudine's room. One of them calls out:

'Monsieur, Monsieur! Come quickly!'

Édouard rushes up, sees Claudine fainted on her bed, goes back down and forces the door open with his shoulder. A long silence. Everyone is huddled in front of the door, the servants and the terrified children. Then, great chaos, children shouting:

'I'm scared! I'm scared! Is she dead?'

We see the living room and the candles on the tree that flicker and go out.

Claudine has opened her eyes. They are alone. He tries to laugh: 'Are you feeling better? You gave me quite a fright, you know, my dear.'

Claudine: 'Oh, why did you wake me up? I was in such a deep sleep.'

'Listen, I'm your friend, a true friend, Claudine . . . Tell me the truth . . . Is what Marie-Laure said true?'

Claudine smiles sadly: 'Ah, so Marie-Laure told you? Yes, it's true.'

Meanwhile, Christiane and Jeannot slip into the empty living room. They are holding a box of matches and light all the candles on the tree again, one by one. They are very excited.

'Wait 'til you see how pretty it will look . . . We didn't get to see it before with all the grown-ups pushing us around! Turn off the lights.'

But once the lights are off, all we see is the bare Christmas tree, bits of streamers and old wrapping paper on the floor.

'Oh!' the children say, sadly.

At that moment, a great commotion. Claudine's parents have been warned and rush into her room. Marie-Laure follows them.

'You miserable child! You have no pity, you don't care at all about your family,' etc.

Édouard: 'Monsieur, may I have the honour of asking for Claudine's hand in marriage?'

Her father (furious): 'Claudine's hand? I . . . yes . . . you can see I'm taken aback . . . I mean, deeply moved . . . (To Claudine, much more gently than before) So, no more foolishness, right? Ah, youth, fortunate youth . . . you get married, you kill yourself, just like that . . . Wait until you're my age, then you'll understand what it means to have real problems in life!'

Marie-Laure to Édouard, frowning, but making an effort in spite of her bad luck: 'Con . . . congratulations . . .'

Édouard (quietly): 'My dear, I prefer . . . someone who is blossoming rather than someone who is withering.'

Marie-Laure (annoyed): 'I don't understand.'

Claudine and Édouard are alone. 'Thank you, my dear

friend,' she says softly. 'I will be ridiculously faithful to you, I swear it.'

We see their two faces. He looks at her, nods his head, brings her hand to his lips. She says quietly, over and over again, her eyes full of tears: 'Thank you for my child.'

Fade out.

That evening. Guests at the dinner table. Her father raises his glass: 'I have the pleasure of announcing the engagement of my daughter Claudine to Monsieur Saulnier.'

A discreet murmur of congratulations.

One lady to her mother: 'You must be very happy!'

'Oh, naturally, but it's so sad to lose one's children, and mine are still such babes . . . So when we send them out into the world all alone for the first time, we do worry so, don't we?'

Everyone leaves the table. Everything is discreet, proper. The servants walk by in silence, serving the coffee. On the sad Christmas tree, the candles have nearly burned out on its broken branches.

Jeannot and Christiane's room; they are in bed. We hear the nanny snoring. Little Jeannot is asleep, clutching his toys to his heart. Christiane, sitting on her bed, is crying softly; she wipes away her tears. Jeannot wakes up and whispers: 'Why are you crying?'

Christiane (pitifully): 'I don't know . . .'

Jeannot: 'Oh, but didn't you have a good time today? The Christmas tree, and now Claudine is going to get married . . . I'll be the ring bearer and you'll be the flower girl . . . didn't you have a good time?'

Christiane shakes her head.

'Why?'

Christiane buries her face in her pillow.

'Because . . . I don't know . . .'

Silence.

Faint melancholic music gradually fades away:

> *Childhood, Innocence, Dawn of the world . . .*
> *Dawn of love*
> *The most wonderful days . . .*

1932

PAUL ARÈNE (1843–1896) was a poet, playwright and author of fiction from Provence in southern France who contributed articles and stories to Paris newspapers.

JEAN-PHILIPPE BLONDEL was born in 1964 in Troyes, France, where he lives as an author and English teacher. He has published nearly a dozen novels, including *The 6:41 to Paris,* published in English translation by New Vessel Press. It has been a bestseller in both France and Germany.

FRANÇOIS COPPÉE (1842–1908) was a poet, playwright and short story writer. He was also an anti-Semitic activist involved in the campaign for legal persecution of French army officer Alfred Dreyfus on baseless allegations of treason.

ALPHONSE DAUDET (1840–1897) was a native of Provence who wrote comic novels and other works of fiction that depict Parisian social and professional life. Daudet was notoriously anti-Semitic, and counted among his friends Édouard Drumont, founder of the National Anti-Semitic League of France, and publisher of an inflammatory tract, *La France juive*. Daudet also wrote extensively about his experience living with syphilis.

ANTOINE GUSTAVE DROZ (1832–1895), born in Paris and son of a sculptor, trained as a visual artist and later wrote stories about family life and psychological novels.

DOMINIQUE FABRE, born in 1960, writes about people living on society's margins. He is a lifelong resident of Paris. Two of his novels have been translated into English, including *Guys Like Me*, which was published in 2015 by New Vessel Press.

ANATOLE FRANCE (1844–1924), was a bestselling author, poet and journalist. He was awarded the Nobel Prize for Literature in 1921 after writing novels of social and political satire. France's story 'The Juggler of Notre Dame,' is based upon a medieval legend. This religious miracle tale is similar to the later Christmas carol, 'The Little Drummer Boy.'

ANATOLE LE BRAZ (1859–1926) was known for his poetry, novels and collections of folklore legends from his native Brittany. He recorded the songs of Breton peasants and fishermen in a volume awarded a prize by the Académie Française.

GUY DE MAUPASSANT (1850–1893) is considered a master of the short story. He studied law and worked as a civil servant before coming under the tutelage of Gustave Flaubert. As Flaubert's protégé, he was introduced into an authors' circle including Émile Zola and Ivan Turgenev. Maupassant wrote over three hundred stories, travel books, and six novels, including *Bel-Ami* and *Pierre et Jean*.

IRÈNE NÉMIROVKSY (1903–1942) was born in Kiev into a Jewish banking family. Following the Bolshevik Revolution, she moved to France and wrote in French. Némirovsky was baptised as a Catholic in 1939, three years before her arrest and deportation to Auschwitz where she died. Her best-known novel, *Suite Française*, was published posthumously and translated into English by Sandra Smith.

'Christmas in Algiers'
translated by Warren Barton Blake

'The Juggler of Notre Dame'
translated by Anna C. Brackett

'St Anthony and His Pig'
translated by J. M. Lancaster

'The Lost Child'
translated by J. Matthewman

'The Louis d'Or'
'A Christmas Supper in the Marais'
'Salvette and Bernadou'
'I Take Supper with My Wife'
translated by Antoinette Ogden

'Noël'
translated by Sandra Smith

'Christmas Eve'
translated by Frederick Caesar de Sumichrast

'The Wooden Shoes of Little Wolff'
'A Miracle'
translator unknown

'The Gift'
'Christmas at the Boarding School'
translated by Michael Z. Wise

Discover more Vintage Christmas Tales...

penguin.co.uk/vintage-classics